A Feast of Tales

A Feast of Tales

(Gently twisted)

Dawn Bush

Bridge House

British Library Cataloguing in Publication Data
A Record of this Publication is available from the British
Library

ISBN 978-1-914199-30-1

This edition published 2022 by Bridge House Publishing
Manchester, England

Contents

The Frog Prince

Ferdy lay flat on his stomach gazing longingly at the slug as it slimed its way across the damp flagstones of the courtyard. His tongue poked swiftly but uselessly out of his mouth a couple of times, then he put his chin on his hands and sighed.

"Is your Highness quite well?"

The voice came from behind his head, making him jump. He scrambled to his feet and, trying not to feel sheepish, looked into the face of the Valet of the Prince's Chamber who had crept up behind him. He gathered all his courage: for once he was going to give the servant a piece of his mind.

"I wish you wouldn't do that! I haven't got eyes in the back of my head you know!"

"Of course not, your Highness. Whoever heard of such a thing?"

Ferdy could have bitten his tongue out. He lowered his eyes so he couldn't see the look of sly disdain in the servant's eyes. Nobody could guess how much he missed the ability to see all around him without moving his head, but even so it wasn't the most subtle rebuke he could have chosen. Also, as usual, the sharpness of the comment as it had sounded in his head was lost on the way out of his throat. The bobbing of his over-large Adam's apple as he swallowed gave the impression he was nervous, and truth to tell, he often was. He had underestimated how much he had grown accustomed to pond life, and this environment seemed alien to him now, far more than he had ever believed possible when, full of courage and determination, he had wooed the spoilt Princess Isadora in the most unusual and successful way.

In the general way of things, the idea of a frog winning the heart of a brat of a princess by finding her golden ball and insisting on sharing her pillow as a reward was outrageous, and would no doubt be considered by your average bloke to be a blessed stroke of good fortune: but this was fairyland, where anything could happen – and not all of it beneficial.

The valet bowed in an exaggerated fashion, the depth of his bow somehow managing to convey superiority rather than deference. "Her Royal Highness the Princess Isadora requests that you return to the castle to dress for dinner."

"I know, I know, I was just coming," said Ferdy, crossly. He pushed past the servant and strode across the courtyard muttering under his breath, "Pompous old jackass. Why can't he just say, 'Your wife is looking for you; dinner's nearly ready'? What's so hard about that?"

Ferdy hated dressing for dinner. He hated the long banqueting table, frequently bursting with people sitting shoulder to shoulder, with Isadora at one end and himself at the other. He resented the fact that they were hardly ever alone, and he had to struggle to converse with some female he didn't know – and didn't want to know. They either giggled and wouldn't look at him or talked loudly about subjects that bored or embarrassed him. There had even been one spinster of a certain age who had asked him in a not very subtle whisper about the mating habits of frogs.

Even on the rare evenings that they were alone, Isadora insisted on retaining their places at the head and the foot of the table; she said it was the proper thing to do. Well, Ferdy was fed up with doing the proper thing. He decided that it was time he asserted himself.

The gong sounded, and Ferdy marched into the dining room determined to claim his place next to his wife: but as he burst through the door, he realised his plans were already scuppered. Both places were taken. On Isa's right hand sat her disapproving Father: on the left—

"Well, I'm blowed!"

Ferdy's eyes lit up as he recognised his Fairy Godmother. "If it isn't old Fairy Fenella!"

He leapt up and down for a moment, then remembering what, as well as where, he was, he bowed impeccably before throwing off restraint and giving her a smacking kiss on either cheek.

"Less o' the old, frog-face," she said, her strident accent disagreeing with the polite flow of small talk from the other diners.

"Don't call him that," snapped Isadora.

Fenella looked at Isadora, narrowing her eyes.

"– er – please," added the Princess, in milder tones.

"What brings you to this neck of the woods?" asked Ferdy. "I mean, not that I'm not glad to see you but…" He tipped an inebriated Earl off the chair next to her, lowering his voice as he continued, "…why on earth would anyone *choose* to come here if they don't have a good reason?"

The Earl, finding himself on his feet and his chair now occupied, scratched his head and wandered off in the direction of the wine waiter.

Fairy Fenella smiled and patted Ferdy's knee. "I wanted to see 'ow my little lamb chop was doin'."

"Oh," said Ferdy, not very convincingly, "I'm alright, you know."

"Happy?" she asked.

"Ye-es -" he said.

Fenella continued looking.

"Yes," he said firmly. "I love Isadora very much. I'm very grateful to you for the help you gave me in bringing us together."

Fenella squinted at him, but still said nothing.

Ferdy sighed. "I never could hide anything from you, could I, Godma? If you must know, I miss… I miss… He

8

took a deep breath and burst out: "I miss having slugs for supper!"

Unfortunately, just at that moment there was a natural lull in the conversation, and the statement, bursting from him with the pent-up pain and frustration of months of misery, resounded around the room with disastrous clarity.

"Ferdy!" hissed Princess Isadora, as the guests collapsed into laughter. "Haven't I told you never to mention your former life? Never!"

She picked up the soup spoon by her plate and began to hit him with it.

"Never, never, never," she chanted, punctuating each remark with a swipe.

"You total moron," she continued as the guests tried unavailingly to curb their hilarity. "You've undone months of hard work, months! Now we're going to have to start all over again."

"Start with what?" asked Fenella, who was noting the princess' behaviour with interest.

"With a whole new publicity campaign," said Isadora, excitedly.

"We've employed this wonderful PR person, Justin Makepiece, and Ferdy has a whole new image. They've even faked photos of him growing up as a prisoner in a castle made of ice. The angle is that my eyes, burning with love for him, melted the ice with one hot glance. It's the talk of the kingdom."

Isadora rattled on oblivious as Fenella's eyes narrowed dangerously. "And of course we make sure he's never snapped near ponds, streams or drains. The paparazzi are everywhere so we have to be very vigilant. It's quite a tough job."

"I'm sure," murmured Fenella.

The king, whose long experience made him a little more

sensitive to the whimsical moods of menopausal fairies, broke in diplomatically.

"You see," he said in a conciliating tone, "it had to be done, my dear fairy. The kingdom wouldn't have had it. We'd be a laughing-stock from the Snow Queen's palace to Puss in Boots' barley fields. I mean to say, a frog, you know? Now, a bear, or a beast, or even a poor Chinaman with a lamp; those are all politically acceptable; but – a frog? A frog who, as a man, has an unfortunately big adam's apple, a weedy voice and a predilection for jumping up and down when excited…" He shook his head gravely. "No, Madam, even you must admit, we had to do something. Very grateful and all that, nothing personal against poor old Ferdy, but we couldn't just leave him as he was."

"Are you staying the night, Godma?" asked Ferdy, trying to move the conversation on to safer ground.

"She is not," said Isadora. "I already offered."

"Changed my mind," snapped Fenella. "Could do with a change of scene. I'll 'ave the second best guest bed, if you don't mind, Belladonna."

"It's Isadora," said Isadora, flatly.

"Ok Isa*dooor*a, whatever you say, but the second-best guest bed if you don't mind. The first one is too close to your Pa's room. Last time I stayed he lost his way in the dark and I found him curled up in my bed wearing my Winnie-the-Pooh pyjamas. It was very disconcertin'. They were never the same afterwards."

"Neither was I," muttered the king under his breath, stroking his head tenderly at the memory. "That chamber pot could have done me a serious injury."

Fenella got up.

"I'm going to bed now," she said; "but I just want you to remember this. Ferdy was a frog for a long time. He was a good frog, and a kind frog, but he was a frog; and while he was a frog, I loved him and nurtured him and brought him to you for a good life. Take care, Isadora Belladonna, because I could quite easily make him a frog once again, and if I did, well…" She came so close to Isadora that they were nose to nose, "…well, I might just remember that a wife's place is by her husband's side. Then you'd have something to croak about, wouldn't you?"

She tapped Isadora on the arm in a friendly fashion and turned to Ferdy.

"Godson," she said in a false posh voice. "Wud you cah to accompany me to may chamber? Ay thank you most kindly."

Alone in Fenella's room the two of them looked at each other.

"It hasn't worked out quite as we expected, has it, Ferdy?" said the fairy.

"No, Godma, but I think that's my fault. I'm just not comfortable as a human being anymore. This is the life I thought I wanted: but truth to tell – I got used to being a frog, and it isn't as easy as I thought trying to get back to being a handsome prince."

"That little madam doesn't deserve you. I wish I'd never pushed you her way, but I thought you could help each other. This is fairyland after all, where anything can happen – and as we can see, not all of it beneficial." She sighed. "I suppose I thought you'd help her be less spoilt and she'd help you have more self-esteem. But it hasn't worked. A spoilt brat she was, and a spoilt brat she remains, and you – well, look at you. You'd be better off without her."

"Don't say that," snapped Ferdy. "You don't know her. You don't know what she's had to put up with, always having to live up to the King's expectations. She did a brave thing marrying me when he wanted Prince Charming on a white steed for his only daughter. And we were happy, for a while. It was only when they hired that wretched PR fellow, Justin. He thinks I'm not good enough. Not good enough for her, not good enough for the Kingdom. And he's right. I'm not."

He looked at Fenella wretchedly.

"Godma," he said, "did you mean what you said in there? About turning me into a frog again?"

She shook her head.

"No," she said, "I wouldn't do it. It really wouldn't be wise: and you know, you did marry her. You are supposed to stick with her now. Whoever heard of an unhappy marriage in fairyland?"

"I suppose not. And I'm not unhappy with Isa, really I'm not. When we're on our own… when we wander down to the pond where we met, and sit in the moonlight together… those are the happiest times I've ever had; but since that Justin fellow came, we've not been allowed near any water, so those times are becoming – well, they're just lovely memories really. I wonder sometimes if she wishes we'd never met, and then I think it would help her if I changed back into a frog."

"Well, like I say, it's possible, but if I were to turn you back, it would not only be dangerous, it would be final. It messes up your metabolism something chronic, shifting back and forth – do it more than twice and you'd end up as a man with frog's legs, or a frog with a man's nose, or something. Anyway, it wouldn't solve matters. She'd still be your wife, only she'd be a Princess married to a frog. Not helpful."

"I suppose not. Well, maybe things'll seem better in the morning. Good night Godma, sleep tight. I'm glad you came. It's good to talk to someone who understands."

"All part of the service, boy," said Fenella, winking at him.

Ferdy didn't feel like going to bed. The guests would be here for a while longer, dancing and partying for at least another hour. It was one of the things he resented; that their time wasn't their own, that they were continually at the beck and call of the party scene, and that even their nights off were about how to promote the image of a well-bred couple. It made them sound like a pair of horses. Spying the Earl – now completely plastered – going into the ballroom, he slipped out of a side door into the palace grounds and started to walk. The night was balmy, with a few fine shreds of mist whispering their way across the creamy moon; the stars peeked out from small bundles of rebellious cloud; the mountains stood hunched on the horizon, neatly rolled and folded like picturesque bedding. The air smelt delicious as the plants released their night scents, wooing the moths with their honeyed breath. Ferdy walked aimlessly, just enjoying being there, until he realised that his feet had unconsciously taken him to his favourite place: the pond where he and Isa had first met. He stood for a while, drinking in the sounds and scents. He was so deep in thought he didn't hear the footsteps behind him.

"I thought I might find you here. Did you have an enlightening conversation with your interfering old Godmother?"

Ferdy frowned. "At least she cares about me, Isa. You don't. I thought you did once, but you don't, do you?"

Isadora turned her head away to hide her unshed tears. Trying not to cry always made her sound shrewish. "Is that what you think?"

"Well, you seem intent on changing me into something I'm not."

"You did it once, Ferdy, so I could love you. Do it again."

"You're wrong, Isa. You loved me before, when I was still a frog. It took some time, but in the end you loved me because we were best friends before anything else. When I was a frog you trusted me enough to let me sleep on your pillow, and you told me everything; all your troubles, all your hopes and plans. As you went to sleep, I was so near to you I could hear your dreams. We were so close, Isa. What happened? What changed?"

She sighed. "You did, Ferdy. You did."

"What?"

"You don't understand. While you were a frog and my best friend, it didn't matter. When you changed into a man, and as a man you married me, well, all the stuff that didn't matter for a frog started to matter for a Prince. You didn't just marry me, you married my family, my position as Princess of the kingdom. You married the life I lead as the King's only daughter. How could we know you would need to change even more? I wish that meddling old Godmother of yours had done the whole job and changed your nature as well as your appearance. You just don't fit, Ferdy, and it kills me every time I see someone smirk at you, or mimic you behind your back. It kills me when they mutter about the way you walk, or the way you dress. It kills me when they find something to mock about everything you do. I can't bear it, Ferdy. I just can't bear it. I wish you'd stayed a frog. Better still, I wish we'd never met!"

She turned and ran away before he could see the tears rolling down her cheeks. He shouted after her, "Isadora, don't go! Isa– Oh, it's hopeless!"

A voice came out of the darkness. "It certainly looks that way."

"Who's that? Who's been eavesdropping?" Ferdy peered into the shadowy shrubs.

"Eavesdropping? Not at all, dear boy. Just doing my

job. I followed you to make sure you didn't wander near the water. You've already done enough damage for one day."

Ferdy sighed. "Oh Justin. It's you. I might have known."

"Can't keep away from that smelly old pond, can you? Breeding will out, I always say. You can't make a silk purse out of a sow's ear, and you can't make Prince Charming out of a frog."

"Yes, well, there's not a lot you can do about it is there?"

"Well now, that's just where you're wrong. You heard what she said. She loved you more when you were a frog. Wouldn't it be better for both of you if you became a frog again?"

Ferdy shook his head. "I already asked my Fairy Godmother. She said it was too dangerous, and she said it wouldn't make any difference now anyway. She'd be a Princess married to a frog, which is worse."

Justin laughed quietly. "That just shows your Godmother's lack of skill. I have a little magic of my own, you know: PR magic. I can spin a spell or two. A little spin here, and there is no Prince: a little spin there, and there was no marriage. It's all a matter of manipulation. It can be done."

Ferdy was silent.

"Think about it. There's more than one way to turn you back into a frog. Here." He handed Ferdy a little phial. "In here are three drops from the Fire Flowers of Norgon. Swallow the drops under the light of a full moon whilst standing on one leg by a lily pond, and you will be a frog again."

"What do you get out of this? Why do you want me to do it?"

"Me? I don't want you to do anything. I'm just trying to solve a problem. It's what I do. You said you were

15

happier as a frog. Isadora was happier when you were a frog. You do what you think best."

After Justin left, Ferdy sat for a long time by the pond, contemplating the phial in his hand. The moon rose a little higher in the sky and hung there as if waiting for him. Ferdy thought about all that had been said to him, until it seemed to him that there were only two options. He could have a life with Isa, working with her to try and do the best for them both: or he could have a life without her as a simple frog and it would be as if they had never met.

"It's no good," he thought. *"There's no such thing as a happy ever after in this love story. I can't bear the thought of life without her; so, if life with her means life with her family, her position and her PR machine, I guess I'll just have to put up with it."*

With that thought, he tossed the phial towards the shrubbery where it rolled away, chinking gently as it hit a stone.

Meanwhile, Isadora had dried her eyes and was dressing for bed. When the knock came at the door of her bedchamber, she called out to Ferdy, "Come in." When there was no answer, she went over and opened the door impatiently. "Silly boy. I know we've had a bit of a barney, but you don't have to knock– Oh!"

"Yes, darling, it's me." Justin pushed his way past her into her room.

"Well, PR man, this is a little late for a business call. What do you want?"

He laughed. "I thought you would have guessed by now. I'm not really a PR man. I'm Prince Justin from the Norgon kingdom, and I was hired by your Father to sort out your unfortunate situation. You'll be happy to know I've just succeeded."

"What do you mean? How have you succeeded?"

"I've done a little work on your little froggy husband. You're free, Isadora. Free at last to marry me." He grasped her by the hands. "Your husband is down by the pond turning himself back into a frog, and when I've finished, you'll never have to worry about him again." With that he pulled her to him forcefully and kissed her full on the lips.

As she broke away, there was a cry from the doorway. They turned to see Ferdy, his face full of anguish. He took one look at the sight of his wife in the arms of another man, and he turned and ran full pelt back towards the pond.

Isadora screamed.

"You idiot! What have you done?" She pushed Justin away. He grasped her hands again.

"Take your filthy mitts off me, you absolute moron!" Isadora was struggling to pull herself free. "Let me go! Let me go, I said!"

Finding Justin more persistent in his attentions than she could handle, she suddenly remembered Fenella's trick.

"Justin," she panted as he grabbed her more strongly than before, "Justin, I need the pot! I need the chamber pot!"

He took a step back.

"What, now?" he asked.

"Yes, immediately," she replied desperately.

He watched as she picked it up from under the bed. She stood there, pot in hand, looking at him.

"Oh, of course," he said and turned his back…

Isadora sprinted down the Palace grounds in her nightdress, ignoring the flashes of the Paparazzi as they took their opportunities. This was a great night for them. First the Prince, then the PR man in Her Highness' bedchamber, and then the Princess, clad in her honeymoon lingerie, haring it off down the garden. Worth a fortune, and it looked like there might be more. Isadora was already gone. They took off after her as one man.

17

It took Ferdy hardly any time to find the phial. He'd heard it chink; it was by the only big stone there was. He wrenched the top off. He glanced at the sky; the moon was still up, but waning. He stood on one leg. One drop… Two drops…

"Ferdy!" Isadora cried. He hesitated. "Ferdy, it's not what you think!"

"How can you deny it? What can you say, Isa? You were kissing him! That – that candidate for a perfume ad was in our bedroom and you were kissing him! With our wedding photograph by the bed! I was right all along; I'll be better as a frog!"

"Ferdy, no!" she screamed as he stood on one leg and lifted the phial. "I wasn't kissing him…"

A blinding light flashed as one of the Paparazzi got the best snap of his career.

"…*he* was kissing *me*," she finished, miserably.

Ferdy croaked.

"Oh, Ferdy." She wept. "Why couldn't you wait? I love you, you idiot! I've always loved you…"

"Well," said Ferdy, some weeks later, "I suppose I ought to have expected this. Where are we going to put them all?"

"Don't worry darling," said Isadora. "There'll be space. And in no time at all, they'll be wanting to leave home."

Ferdy nodded.

"Do you know, Isa," he said, "I've never been happier. You may have been a brat of a princess…"

She giggled, and finished his sentence for him, "…but I make a wonderful frog. I'm going back to the pad. Coming?"

Previously published in the *Alternative Renditions* anthology, Bridge House publishing.

Blind Date

The woman locked the door of the cheap, functional room behind her, still shaking. Her face was pale, with beads of sweat in evidence on her forehead. As she glanced around the room with distaste, the colour came slowly seeping back into her cheeks. Her eyes shed the look of horror and returned to their normal expression; confident, serene and in control. Lost in thought, she leaned on the stained vanity unit, tapping rapidly on it with red-tipped fingers. The moment of decision was evident to anyone who might be watching; but it was wasted, since she was alone in the bathroom: gloriously alone.

Francine was intelligent, erudite, and unfailingly polite. Her analytical brain could deduce how the past hour and a half might have been a genuine mistake: and she was not one to bear grudges unnecessarily. However, a firm stand must be taken, so there could be no further misconstruction.

Having reached her decision, she implemented it swiftly. She dipped into her neat handbag for a pen and a sheet of the subtle but expensive notepaper she always carried In Case of Emergency. Then, seating herself elegantly on the plastic-lidded pedestal, she wrote in a swift and sloping hand that suited her rather old-fashioned way of expressing herself.

Dear Sir,

Since the whole of our brief encounter appears to have been open to severe misinterpretation, I find myself driven to the unusual measure of communicating by letter in order to correct your misguided beliefs.

When you joined me for dinner at The Secluded Chat bistro, I was not wearing the pink carnation in

19

order to identify myself as the first of your blind dates. I had been to my cousin's wedding and had slipped away from the noisy marquee in order to enjoy a quiet lunch alone, since canapés are not to my taste. Your appearance in the chair opposite was a surprise to say the least, which is why I sat with my mouth open for quite thirty seconds. It was not, I'm afraid, because I was struck by your uncanny resemblance to a silver-haired Buddy Holly; although upon reflection I can see why you might think so.

When you took the liberty of ordering for me because, you said, you are such an accurate reader of character, the look that you interpreted as grateful thanks would surely have struck mortal fear into anyone of ordinary sensibility. If you had drawn breath and allowed me a moment in which to expostulate, I am sure you would have understood your mistake immediately. Incidentally, I am allergic to prawns; therefore, you taking the opening of my mouth – which I did with the intention of speaking – as an opportunity to pop several of them in it was the true reason for my gasping for breath, and not, as you supposed, a manifestation of uncontrollable desire elicited by your presence. The protracted interlude in the Ladies which followed was in order to utilise the EpiPen I keep by me for just such an emergency. Unfortunately, the symptoms of anaphylactic shock deprived me of my wits for a period, which is why I could not take the opportunity to leave.

When I attempted to mop up the wine you spilled down me, it was not an invitation for you to remove my silk blouse and replace it with your polyester shirt so that I could have something dry to wear. As your actions resulted in us being expelled from my favourite restaurant, I might conceivably have expected an apology; sadly, the half an hour's osculation to which you subjected me did not serve as such. The sounds you patently interpreted as moans of delight were in reality indignant grunts of protest; and when I stamped on your foot with my stiletto heel I did not apologise, so your protestations of forgiveness for my action – which was not accidental – were superfluous. Unfortunately, the lingering remnants of prawn in your mouth re-ignited the symptoms of anaphylactic shock to a degree which prevented me from protesting against being folded into your taxi, and were still in evidence when you escorted me to your room; these symptoms were not, as you seemed to suppose, the result of imbibing too much wine whilst waiting to meet you. It is, after all, the middle of the afternoon.

I hope that the receipt of this note, which I have taken the opportunity to write whilst powdering my nose in your hotel bathroom, will dispel your supposition that I am here willingly with the express intention of servicing your lust. Since I am now sufficiently recovered from the weakness caused by ingesting the prawns, I would very much appreciate it if, when I unlock the bathroom door, you would grant me unimpeded passage to the hotel lobby, and thence to the outside world.

Yours etc,

Francine (NOT Nancy,)
Your unwilling guest.

Francine folded the note, and getting up from the toilet seat, picked from her handbag a small bottle of cochineal, that she had bought at her sister's request, for use at the wedding in one of her infamous practical jokes. Not being the jesting sort, Francine didn't know what joke was planned; but she decided that the cochineal would work just as well for a mild but effective revenge. Taking the tooth glass, she mixed the cochineal with the small tin of Vaseline she kept – for use in keeping her lips supple – in a compartment of her bag. She removed her stilettos, clambered into the bath, and reached up. Using the plastic bag in which the cochineal had been wrapped to cover her hand, she removed the shower head, filled it with the mixture, and replaced it.

A knock came at the bathroom door, coupled with a shout. "Hey! Are you ok in there, little lady?"

Francine stiffened. Taking the note, she unfolded it and added a postscript. Then she re-folded it and slipped it under the door.

"Awww. You sending me love-notes already? Hey, Nancy, we only just met!"

Francine waited silently in the bathroom whilst her companion, muttering to himself, read her note. Shortly thereafter, she unlocked the door, and without looking at him, exited the bathroom, the room and the sleazy hotel without obstacle.

As she hailed a taxi, she permitted herself a small smile at the memory of her postscript, which she considered to be inspired:

P.S. I wish you luck with this evening's blind date. May I suggest, having perforce been in close proximity to your luxuriant but rather greasy silver hair, that you might wish to wash it? Sincerely, F.

Greater Love

She was standing on a corner in the pouring rain. It wasn't that she was absolutely drenched; everybody had been caught in the sudden downpour. The rain had soaked through her thin dress, making it cling to every curve, but whereas on some women it would be sexy, it made her seem rounder than she really was. She was talking to an unsavoury looking tramp, who was gesturing unsteadily, the spray from his half-empty beer can mingling with the drops of rain, spattering her indiscriminately.

None of this would have drawn Max's attention. He would have put her down as one of that vague army of do-gooders, if he'd thought about her at all. No, there was nothing special about her; but as he passed her on his way home from work, revving the engine to draw out into the main street, his eye captured the scenario and imprinted it on his mind like a photograph. All the way home it kept coming back. Indicate left – there she was. Draw into the lock-up – there she was again. When she popped up unbidden as he was putting on the football, he decided there must be a reason and thought about her for a few seconds; but still he concluded there was nothing special about her and tried to dismiss her from his mind. It wasn't until she interrupted as he was swigging his lager (beer drops and rain spattering mingled over her face) that he caught her expression.

That was it.

It was the expression on her face.

All over town people who had been caught in the flash storm were going about their business. Men in wet shirts that stuck to their backs; women with make-up wiped away in the onslaught; kids in sandals kicking delightedly in puddles whilst mothers tugged them away; but not one of them had that expression on their face. Annoyance, resignation, rueful laughter perhaps: but *she* radiated an expression Max had never seen before. It wasn't spurious sympathy, or condescension. It was nothing he could name, but her face bore a radiance that he recognised somewhere deep inside. Joy? Too strong. Love? Close, but too many connotations. Anyway, who in their right minds would love a lousy stinking tramp? Max forgot about her and went for another beer.

The next time he saw her was on his way between nightclubs. She was serving out some kind of hot drink – soup maybe. It wasn't a salubrious part of town, and though she wasn't alone Max was annoyed with her for putting herself at risk. Asking for it, asking to be raped and murdered, her body left naked and un-mourned near a skip somewhere.

He couldn't concentrate. The music was too loud, the girls too brassy. He went home.

Over the next few weeks, Max discovered that noticing her once had led to him seeing her everywhere; and that every time he saw her, she caught him on some subliminal level. The situation might change, but the radiance shone undimmed from her countenance even when she wasn't smiling.

Her first tentative smile for him wasn't the kind of smile Max was used to, the come-to-bed boldness he expected as his due. When she could no longer doubt he was noticing her, she smiled at him in a vaguely puzzled way, almost as if looking over her shoulder to see who he was really looking at. He found himself dreaming about her at the most inconvenient times – at work, at home, at the match; once even as he was about to bed another girl. He couldn't help himself. He was caught.

Friday night, he finally gave up. The nightclub was

noisy, and there was no point anymore: his chat-up line had lost its edge. He wandered out into the night to where she was handing out soup, dealing with the no-hopers gently but firmly, occasionally smiling, but always wearing that expression that had come to haunt him. The only time she showed any fear was when a couple of youths started to hassle them. Her companion, an older man, quietly started to pack up the things to get out of the way: but he wasn't quick enough. One of them had her pinned against the wall. Once, Max might have laughed; but tonight, he leapt into action.

"Hey! Piss off and leave her alone, pal!"

She looked at him, surprised but grateful, as the gang slunk away muttering threats.

It was three weeks before she took his offer of a date seriously. They were sorting donations at the warehouse. She was working; he, to his own surprise, was volunteering.

"You're just going to keep on asking, aren't you?" She sounded amused rather than annoyed.

"Yep. Until you give me a chance. One chance, that's all."

"Why me?"

"Why not?"

"Oh, you're impossible! Hasn't anyone ever said no?"

"Look, it's only a coffee. Or a movie. Saturday afternoon, broad daylight. I promise I won't be a douche."

"I just don't get why you want to hang out with me."

"Honestly? You intrigue me. I've never met anyone like you. Come on, give yourself a break. You work so hard all the time. It'll be a treat. And if we don't get on, I'll never bother you again. Promise."

She finished packing a box and hefted it on top of the stack. Then she huffed a sigh. "Fine."

"Coffee or a movie?"

"You choose."

"Ok. Both."

"Chancer! I should have known." She softened the words with a smile.

"Ok, Max, Saturday afternoon it is. Movie first, coffee after, and I hold you to your promise. One sign of Max the douchebag and I'm off, ok?"

Max was delighted. It was the first time he'd ever thought of himself as lucky to have a date. As he sat facing her over a cappuccino, he noted that up close, she was a bit older than he had thought at first. That expression held something of the purity of unsullied youth, and it was only now that he could see the lines at the corners of her eyes, and something about her neck that gave away the passing of time. She was thirty-one: three years his senior. It didn't matter. She was fascinating. For the first time since he was fifteen, Max did nothing but talk on a first date; but there was something of a hesitancy about her, something held back. It was odd. She had the demeanour of a young girl, but the wisdom of a woman; and Max had no idea how he should play it. Occasionally, he would catch her looking at him with a puzzled air. When he smiled, she smiled back like a hazy sunrise on a June morning, with all the promise of a glorious summer day. It was like getting a gazelle to trust him. He had to tread so carefully in case she bolted. A movie and coffee after had become a routine before he asked her to dinner. Dinner turned into a weekly event before he asked her officially to be his girl.

He suspected that she wouldn't succumb the first time he asked her to stay, but the last thing he was expecting was the bombshell that was waiting for him.

"Max, we need to talk..."

He wished he could be angry. Anger wouldn't hurt as

26

much as the complete devastation he felt. No-one had ever dumped him before.

She had done it quite gently. "It's not you, Max, it's me. I don't – I can't play these games anymore. I stopped that a long time ago."

"Stopped what?"

She took his hand and turned it over, exposing the skin under his forearm. He didn't resist. The touch of her finger running over the needle marks sent such excitement through him he couldn't think straight.

"I used to be like you, once. You puzzled me at first. You seemed just like the kind of guys I played with. Those guys wouldn't be interested in me now, and I don't know why you are."

Max was surprised by the fierceness of the jealousy that shot through him at the thought of anyone touching her... anyone but him...

"I used to be just like you."

She pulled her sleeve up and offered her forearm for him to inspect. Bewildered, he noted the faint marks that spoke of her past.

"It's not because you're still using – that wouldn't keep me away. I can't commit to you now, because really, I'm dead."

Max felt like he was drowning.

"You've asked me so many times why I live the way I do. It's because I'm dead – or at least, I should be dead."

She leaned forward, lifting his hand and looking into his eyes.

"I'd been going to the soup kitchen to get food. I couldn't afford to eat because I spent all my money on drugs. There was a guy there... he was one of life's good guys, you know? I liked him. He never judged me. He didn't look at me like I was tonight's shag. He just talked to me, accepted me for what I was. He didn't drink, didn't do drugs; he'd never slept around. He was a do-gooder. Usually I despised them, but there was something about him – he was so strong... and... and genuine, I suppose."

Max shivered. She was describing herself.

"One night I went there to get away from someone I'd robbed. They followed me. They watched as I sat drinking my soup with him, talking. When I left, they followed me again; and so did he. When they pulled a gun on me..."

Max nearly cried out. Her grip on his hand was hurting. Her eyes were somewhere else, the expression in them dimmed.

"When they pulled a gun on me, he took the bullet. He took the bullet that was meant for me. They ran... but he died smiling at me."

She lowered his hand on to the table, relaxing her grip. Absently, she stroked his palm.

"It does something to you, when someone dies in your place. Even if that person's life is not good, I'm sure it does something to you. But his life – his life was special. So now I pretend I died that night, and I'm living his life instead of my own. When I come here and love these people, I'm loving them in his place. When I'm helping them, I'm helping them the way he would do if he were still alive. Why should they suffer because that night, he died instead of me?"

Max licked his dry lips.

"If I changed," he began, "would you – would you marry me?"

Even as he said it, he cringed. They were words he'd never wanted to say. She looked at him with tears in her eyes.

"Oh Max, it wouldn't work. You can't change yourself from the outside. Change happens from inside. You'd get bored with me. I'm not into the things you do, and you'd get bored with the things I'm doing. I can't go back; I'm dead to all that."

Max cleared his throat. "It happened. Things happen. You don't have to tie yourself to a dead man's life just because something happened. Isn't that the worst kind of slavery?"

She shook her head, and her face was radiant again. "Slavery? No... No, it's not slavery. It's freedom." She picked up his arm, brushing the marks. "*This* is slavery."

Max tried not to go to the dealers any longer. He was determined to kick it for her sake, to show her he could change. He didn't owe them anything, so the night the youth came for him he wasn't expecting trouble: why should he? He was the golden boy; nothing had ever disturbed his peace. Perhaps it was the loss of income that galled them. Perhaps they thought he'd shop them; or perhaps it was nothing to do with them and he was just unlucky: he never found out. He was just minding his own business at the nightclub – a stag do for a work colleague. He hadn't even realised she was there, but as he tumbled out into the cold night, he saw her. She was on duty as one of the street pastors, hanging around outside to help those too drunk or too high to know what they were doing. Handing out flats to teenaged girls whose stilettos had ended the night dangling from their fingers instead of their feet; getting a taxi home for those too pissed to do it themselves, or for the lone, distraught ones who had fallen out with their friends. He saw her and called to her.

"Max! Max, no!" she shrieked; and at first, he thought the look of horror on her face was directed at him. She ran straight at him and pushed him hard; he saw the knife flash, heard her scream, and as he lay where he'd fallen, he knew she'd taken the blow that was meant for him. She slid down the wall, her hand clutched to her chest. Her cry alerted her companion, who was already calling the police; but Max had seen the blade slide out of her, leaving blood in its wake.

He crawled over, tried frantically to stem the blood, said her name over and over; but he knew it was no good. As she lay dying in his arms, her face shone with the radiance of love; and at last, he knew for certain that the love was for him.

"Change starts from inside, Max," she whispered. "Time to die."

Published online by *Writing Magazine*; placed second in the Love Story competition.

Magnolia and Moonstone

I knew the moment Ruth set eyes on him that he was Trouble.

I don't know how I knew. It wasn't as if she started acting differently, or anything, but I sensed something inside her – her soul, her psyche, whatever. I can't even say it was a difference in our relationship. No growing cold overnight, or anything obvious like that. Anyway, there we were, walking in the park together as usual, quiet, companionable, like every evening for the last three years. I remember she was telling me about some new idea she had for painting the flat, when suddenly she stopped, leaving me dangling amid shades of Magnolia and Moonstone. I looked where she was looking and couldn't see anything unusual; just a few kids shouting as they played on the swings, and a solitary man standing staring vacantly across the river.

I looked back at her, waiting. I didn't need to say anything. She can read me like a book.

"Sorry, Toby," she said, laughing in that wholehearted way she has, showing all her lovely tiny white teeth. "I got distracted for a moment. Where was I? Oh, never mind, I can't remember. Let's go and get some coffee."

I didn't remind her. Well, what do I know about Magnolia and Moonstone? Anyway, it's her flat, not mine. I just live with her; and that's how I like it. She's never made me feel as if it's not my home.

We walked over to The Café and had our usual – Cappuccino for her, Yorkshire Tea for me (white, no sugar) – and as I watched her playing with the lumps in the sugar bowl, I could see that she was distracted. I was just about to ask what the matter was, when she started to talk about work, and this awful new manager that was making her life a misery. She poured her heart out to me, and I listened as always, and that was it. We went home, snuggled ourselves around each other, and spent the evening watching repeats of Friends. Everything the same, except... Oh, I don't know...

We've been an item ever since we first met, Ruth and me. I can't remember a time when I haven't totally adored her. It's as if my life began the day she first looked into my eyes and whispered my name: Toby. It doesn't sound quite the same on anyone else's lips, but she says it like a caress. And Ruth? She fell for my big brown eyes... so she told me. I think there's more to it than that, though. I seem to be able to sense her moods. I know when to leave her alone, and when to make a fuss of her. I know when she needs a cuddle, and when she needs to get out and blow the cobwebs away. It isn't often spoken, but it's understood: we love each other. It's almost as if there's an invisible cord holding us together. She looks to me for love, companionship and protection: and I look to her for – for – well, let's be honest; she means everything to me. When she looks at me with love in her eyes, it's like I know my reason for being; and when she's unhappy, my world falls apart, and I would do anything to take her troubles on my own back.

I don't want you to think I'm living in cloud cuckoo land. You see, I know she loves me, too. I'm not a fantasist, or a mad stalker, or anything. She loves me. There's no more wonderful feeling than when she takes my face in her gentle hands, looks into my eyes, and says, "Oh, Toby, I do love you. Whatever would I do without you?"

That's why it's so odd that I'm in this predicament.

The next day was like any other. We walked together in the park, laughing at the ducks and their stupid antics, ambling around to see what there was to see. It was a beautiful autumn evening, one of the last of the year: the trees had dressed themselves in their finest array as if they knew the winter winds would come soon to rob them of all their glorious colour. All was as it should be, until we bumped into that man. I recognised him at once. It was the man I'd seen staring vacantly across the river.

I felt Ruth start to shake, and she laughed nervously.

"Toby, this is Matt, my new manager. Matt, this is my-my-" she hesitated a moment before saying firmly, "-my best friend Toby."

"Hi, Toby," said Matt, in a friendly voice: but he was looking at Ruth. My hackles started to rise.

"Would you like some coffee?" he said.

"Oh, thanks," said Ruth, with that pathetic nervous giggle. "Toby and I were just on our way there, weren't we, Toby?"

I nodded grimly, determined not to show that I was hurt. The Café was our special place. No one had ever joined us for coffee before.

I sat there letting my tea grow cold as Ruth chatted to Matt, becoming more and more at ease with him all the while. I watched her laugh her wholehearted laugh – the one that showed all her beautiful tiny white teeth – only this time, it was for him, not for me. My heart felt like a stone.

After that, it became quite a habit for Matt to bump into us just as we were going for coffee: every evening without fail, in fact, until the nights grew dark and the weather turned. At last, I thought, I'll have her all to myself again: but it didn't work out that way at all.

One evening, not long after The Café had shut down for the winter, she came home, and instead of eating with me, left straight away.

"I have to pop out for a while, Toby. Will you be ok on your own? You can listen to the radio, can't you?"

I nodded, dumbstruck. She was going out – without me!

It was on the tip of my tongue to ask where she was going – and more importantly, who she was going with – but I don't own her, after all. What right do I have to interrogate her? I'm not one of those losers that has to dog their girl's every move. I'm secure enough in her love for me for her to have the odd night out with her work friends if she likes.

If only I'd known where my laid-back attitude would lead.

She was late coming in. To be honest with you, I was nearly frantic with worry, though I tried to be cool.

"Oh Toby, you shouldn't have waited up, you silly thing. You must be dog-tired! I'm sorry. Next time, you should just go to bed without me."

I tried to tell her how worried I'd been, but she wasn't listening. In fact, she got a little impatient with me.

"Oh for goodness' sake, Toby, do stop making so much fuss! I'm here, I'm back, I'm not going to leave you! Now just stop it and let me go to bed!"

We went to bed as usual, but instead of cuddling up to me, she pushed me away, muttering that I was invading her personal space. There was nothing I could do but accept it. I spent the whole night wide awake, with no solace for my aching heart but to watch her sleep. Watching her breath rise and fall… watching the shadows from the street lamp play on her beautiful, beloved face, her blonde hair falling across the pillow like rays of pale spring sunshine. Watching until the lazy dawn awoke yawning, peeping in through her bedroom window; and all the time I watched, I knew that I had lost her, that I would never again be the sole comfort of her life. I didn't cry – it would have woken her – but my heart broke that night.

For the next few months, I just took whatever affection she could spare. I know you probably think I should have had more pride – after all, she was treating me no better than a dog – but I loved her so much, I couldn't bear the thought of leaving her. Matt took more and more of her attention. One evening, she even forgot to get me any supper, and I had to fend for myself. I mean, I'm perfectly willing and capable, but she liked to get supper for me, and I was quite happy to let her, so I suppose I'd got into the habit. When she came back, she was mortified, and insisted on getting me something there and then, so I didn't bother to tell her I'd sorted myself out. She never missed the bacon; I think she'd forgotten it was there, and it's against my nature to refuse a second meal. Anyway, food doesn't seem to go anywhere on me. I burn it up, I suppose.

Our relationship limped along for a while, until the day came that she broke the awful news.

"Toby, it's time for a few changes. I'll come straight to the point. As my best friend, you are the first to know. Matt's asked me to marry him: and I've said yes."

From that day on, she banished me from her bedroom.

"You're going to have to get used to sleeping alone, Toby. Matt doesn't approve of dogs on the bed."

It was like a death knell. I've never been her dog; I've always been her best friend. I looked at her reproachfully, but she put on that frowny face she uses when she's trying to show me who's boss, so I slunk into a corner and put my chin on my paws. All night I lay there, confused and alone for the first time in three years. I'd have liked to sleep, but you can't bring sleep by sniffing the wind; if it comes, it comes, and that night it didn't. I know she didn't sleep well either, because in the morning she put sugar in my tea by mistake. She blamed me for it. She said it was my crying that kept her awake, but I know better. You can't share a bed with someone for that long and then suddenly choose to sleep alone. Can you blame me if I whimpered a little? I've never known her be so hard hearted, but because I love her, I had to let her go. Her happiness means more to me than my own; and there was no getting away from the fact that she was blissfully happy. Eventually she packed her stuff and moved into a big house overlooking the park, and though I have a place of my own on their patio, I've never been allowed in her bed again. There's no room for me now that *he's* there.

As for me, my feelings for her haven't changed. She will always be my world, and for her sake, I've even got used to *him*. He tries to bribe me with bones and biscuits, but I have him sussed. I may accept them, but he'll never really win me over. I'm playing a waiting game. The day will come when the novelty will wear off, and she'll notice me again; and then Ruth and me, we'll take our walks in the park to mull over life, love, Magnolia and Moonstone; the way it always used to be.

The Ormolu Clock

Dispassionately, I consider the gaping hole before me. The clay that forms its walls is smooth and sticky, with faint lines down it that speak of the well-used spade that dug it. I can smell damp earth: it reminds me of springtime in the potting shed. Incongruous that it should smell of life. The plain wooden casket rests neatly at its base with barely a few inches to spare, so well does Tom Abbot know his job. He should do; he's been doing it since he was sixteen. Rheumatism makes him slow, but not the less accurate for all that. Dead accurate, comes the thought, and a tight little smile turns up the corners of my cracked lips. I force them down again. It won't do to be caught smiling.

I gaze on, dreaming of warm toast and a cup of tea as the voice of the compassionate young vicar drones in the background. As I watch, Uncle steps forward and rains a little handful of dark earth on the light wood of the casket lid.

It sounds like hail on the shed roof.

It makes me start a little. I wonder where Uncle John got the earth. It's loose, not sticky. Perhaps it's some of the topsoil from his prize garden; or maybe even a bit of compost from the heap that's lain obsolete behind Gran's shed for a year. Wasteful, he would say. Such a sentimental thought would never voluntarily enter his head. Someone must have told him it was the thing to do.

Thinking of Uncle John, I get ready for the inevitable struggle. Not much longer now, and I can have my cup of tea.

Uncle's house is like him, roomy and cold: in the end, the tea is only lukewarm. The fire, inadequately stoked for such a large room, loses its poor heat as Father stands before it, warming his backside at the expense of the rest of us. He is holding forth with one of his salty jokes. Ill-judged, I think: but then, it's not his mother whose death we're celebrating.

When the first voice comes, close to my ear, it makes me jump.

"I was watching you, you hard-hearted bitch. You never shed a single tear. Not one drop."

I put down my cup, so that my brother can't take note of how my hand is shaking.

"So where is it then?" he continues.

I'm not good at pretending, so I don't. "Why are you asking me, particularly?"

He gives me a disbelieving look. "I should think the answer to that is obvious, even to you."

I ponder for a moment, deciding how best to catch him off guard.

"Tell me, James, when did you last see Gran?"

He shrugs. "I don't know. Two, maybe as much as three years ago. Why?"

"Did you see her laid out?"

"No," he says, not getting it.

I raise my eyebrows. "You didn't go to say goodbye? You do surprise me."

"No." He's defensive now. "I didn't want to remember her dead."

My words are like swords. I choose, deliberately. "I prefer to remember her dead."

My lips slide upwards at the corners.

He doesn't like what I've said. He doesn't understand it.

"You've changed, Teeda," he says, shaking his head. "You used to be a nice person."

"You're wrong," I reply. "I wasn't nice. I just kept quiet."

He's not deflected. He grasps my arm. It hurts.

"Just remember; it's mine. You know that. You were there when she promised it to me, weren't you?"

I nod. He glares at me for a moment, then turns away.

I look around at the assembled company: not a large crowd. Mostly family. Aunt Jane sitting on the edge of the leather armchair, the sympathetic look fixed like polygrip on her face, nodding her head as if she's really attending to Mother. Mother, holding forth to anyone who'll listen, the bereaved daughter with the sherry bottle at her elbow like a sentinel on duty. The tears will be displayed when the bottle is half empty. I have no idea whether Mother's grief is real; but it's called for, so it will be properly displayed. Uncle John, playing the role of head of the family to a nicety; the cousins, pale and muted in their dark garb, talking in hushed tones; Aunt Sarah looking as if she wishes she were somewhere else; and Uncle Vic, laughing too loudly at Father's joke.

"Teeda! Nice to see you again. Sorry it's under such sad circumstances."

It's cousin Philip. Philip was in love with me once, years ago, when we were teenagers.

"Hallo, Phil."

"How's the tea?" he asks, for something to say.

"Cold," I reply.

"You're the one I feel for, more than all the others. You were the one who was closest to her at the last. Were you at the house when they came to take her in to hospital?"

"No. I chose that week to go on a course."

That week of all weeks.

Frank, the odd job man, found her. Two days, she'd lain on the floor while I was away, the fall having broken her hip. He found her, in a pool of mess. Frank. He was the window cleaner, really, but he was always in and out of the house, fixing the washers on her taps, making sure she had enough coal to last, mending the loose stair rods so she didn't fall down the stairs, passing the time of day so she didn't feel too lonely. He called the ambulance and stayed with her, holding her hand until she was settled. By the time I came back, the shock had had its effect, and she was already on her way out.

I don't tell Phil that.

"Awful for you," he says, jovially. "I expect you'll miss the old bat."

Will I miss the old bat? Will I miss her, grumbling, getting tipsy, calling her children to hell? Will I miss her two-fingered gestures at the TV? Will I miss her meanness, her bitterness, her loneliness? Taken aback, I haven't a cynical reply to hand, and he takes advantage of my weakness.

"By the way, do you know who's got that useless old clock she had? I looked for it when I was down there yesterday, but it's not there."

Ah.

"I haven't been in the house for a while," I reply, knowing his tactics now. "It was there when I was there last."

"Where was it?"

"Where it always was. She kept it on top of the bureau."

"The pine bureau? It's not there now. Someone else must have picked it up." He ponders for a moment, as though deciding whether to speak. Can he trust me to understand his motivation in asking for it? It's not his true motivation, but he wishes it were.

"You see, it's rather awkward, but I really would like to have it. She promised it to me years ago, as a memento. Told me ever since I was a child that it would be mine one day." He smiles tentatively. "You do understand, don't you, Teeda?"

40

"Of course," I say, and I do.

"Well, if you find out who has it, will you tell them? I wouldn't insist, except that it was her wish that I should have it."

I nod graciously. Of course I will tell them. What harm can it do?

He smiles, offers to get me more tea. It's an excuse; he's said what he wanted to say. I'm of no more use to him.

Uncle John comes up.

"Theresa, dear girl, you look frozen. Have some more tea, or would you prefer a sherry?"

Mother sits there with her legs half open. She's still talking non-stop. The tears are flowing freely down her face. She's dabbing at them with her black chiffon scarf.

No, I wouldn't like a sherry.

"Nothing, thank you," I say. My voice sounds frozen, too. Then he attacks, and his attack is more direct than Phil's.

"Now, dear girl, where is the Ormolu clock?"

I shrug. "It was there when I left."

"Ah. That's strange. It isn't there now. I wonder who's got it?"

"I don't think you're alone in wanting to know that."

"Well, if you find out, can you let me know? By rights, you see, it should go to the head of the family. It's an heirloom: quite valuable in its way. Been in the family for generations." He pauses.

I'm not fooled for a moment. "Did she promise it to you, Uncle John?"

"Not in so many words, you know, but I am the head of the family now. It's my responsibility to keep it for the next generation."

I wonder what the family think of that. He's looking at me speculatively, chewing his lip.

"If I'd been sensible, I would have taken it when I was

41

there last year. I could see she was beginning to fail, even then; but the old girl was so possessive of it."

The old girl. The old bat.

"It needs to be taken to a proper menders." He leans into me, invading my space. "Whoever has it is technically guilty of theft, you know."

I smile tightly. "That may be true, but it isn't mentioned in the will. It's part of the other effects. Other effects to be divided, the will says..." He can't dispute me: he hasn't seen the will. "..and you know the old saying, Uncle: 'possession is nine points of the law.' "

I turn my back on him and go up to the fire in a futile effort to thaw myself. Dad is still hogging all its meagre warmth. He turns to me and winks. "Your Uncle been asking you about the clock, has he?"

I nod, keeping my face free from expression.

"Very astute of you to realise the vultures would descend as soon as the old battleaxe was dead. Where have you put it?"

I gaze at him, wondering not for the first time how I come to be of his get.

"If I had taken it and hidden it, as you seem to suppose, what makes you think I would choose to let you into the secret?"

He looks uncomfortable for a moment. "But Teeda, you know she always meant your Ma to have it. She knew John wouldn't value it properly. She promised it to us time and time again. I think she secretly knew that John was only after her money, that's all he's ever been interested in, but your Ma..." He looks over at her, "...your Ma's got a tender heart. She wants it for the memories."

I follow the line of his gaze. Mother is showing Aunt Jane the ruby brooch she is wearing. The expression on her face is nothing so much as smug.

42

"She shouldn't be short of memories. She's already got all of Gran's jewellery."

"Yes, but there's nothing of real value among it, Teeda. Only paste, most of it. She's not being greedy, or anything."

Is she not?

"Of course not," say I.

"So…"

"So?" I echo.

He's annoyed now. "Well, if you're going to be awkward, there's no more to be said: but if you've got it, girl, you'll never have the pleasure of it. I'll be looking for it every time I visit you."

His thrust goes wide. He hasn't visited me so far. I take leave to doubt he'll start now. Disgruntled, he moves away from the fire. At least now its mottled warmth is opened up to everyone. I move away from it as well, suddenly tired. Father and Uncle John are talking, looking in my direction. I can see them enlisting the help of Uncle Vic. As they advance on me together, I decide that the best form of defence is attack.

"Did you see her laid out?" I ask.

"I didn't," says Dad.

"Nor did I, nor did any of us," says Uncle, "but that's not important, Theresa."

"I did," say I. "I said goodbye. But it was too late. She wasn't there to hear it."

James is there, behind them.

"She asked me that question too." He looks at me, hard. I can see something click. "Oh, I get it."

Suddenly they're all too clever, putting two and two together, and there's outrage in the room.

"That sly old witch! She had it buried with her! That's where it is, isn't it? Theresa, isn't it? The sly old witch has got it even now, six feet underground!"

Aunt Sarah's cool voice breaks in. "Best place for it too, if you ask me. Perhaps she knew you would all end up fighting over it."

John snorts. "Not her! The greedy old cow just wanted to take it with her, that's all."

I hold Aunt Sarah's eyes for a moment. A sad little smile touches her lips. A companionable smile. She knows what I'm about.

She saw Gran laid out, too.

The next day, I walk up to Frank's little cottage with the payment in my hand. He opens the door, inviting me in, his smile warm and friendly. The room is small and welcoming; a blazing fire roars in the grate. I apologise for being late paying Gran's debts.

"Oh, no, Theresa, don't worry. Your Gran paid me herself, really. It wasn't about money, for me. I'd rather have something to remember her by than money, anyway."

I see the clock almost straight away, ticking steadily on his mantlepiece as if it has never been broken. There is a sheen on it the like of which I have never seen. He sees my gaze.

"They won't mind that she gave it to me, will they, the family, I mean? If it means something to anyone, I wouldn't like to rob them of it. I wouldn't have taken it at all, only she was so insistent. She was getting quite distressed about it, so I thought it better to give way. I think the poor old lady must have known she hadn't long."

I look at his face. His eyes make you want to smile at him.

"You fixed it," I say.

He raises his eyebrows. "Me? No. I only cleaned it and wound it up. Works a treat now, doesn't it?"

He looks at me.

"Would you like it back, Theresa? I know you'll miss her."

44

Will I miss her? The old bat, the old witch? The battleaxe, the greedy old cow? The poor old lady who was all of this, but who most of all was my Gran?

"I won't miss her last weeks of suffering, Frank."

Fleetingly, unwillingly, I remember those final days in hospital when she didn't even know me. Days when she grew thin and gaunt, and when, thinking herself at home, she offered me tea from a kettle that wasn't there. One day soon I'll remember her in the potting shed, her tender plants and me all secure in her care as the fierce hail bounces off the roof; but for now, my memories of her are not pleasant. I'm not even tempted. I smile at this man: this ordinary man who showed my cantankerous old Granny real honest-to-God love in the last days of her life. I touch his arm.

"No, Frank," I say. "You keep it. She gave it to you, so she must have wanted you to have it. Don't worry about the rest of the family."

The clock sits there quietly, ticking, ticking, ticking.

"No," I say, "they don't care at all."

Walking with Rose

I never even thought about that woman Rose Dolan until one day down the pub, some posh bird asked me why I kept glowering at her. At Rose, I mean. I didn't get what she was on about. I don't glower. but then I realise Posh Bird was right. I prob'ly was frowning a bit, 'cos I realised she annoyed the heck out of me, no idea why. I tried, one time, to work out why I disliked her, taking all her faults one by one – as if each separate thing wasn't enough to tick me off on its own.

Take last summer, for instance, when she ran the stall by mine at the Fête. (I'm retired now, so I do that now and again, just to be congenial, like.) By the time I'd arrived, her table was already set out with its prissy little canopy, those things she calls Preserves all in neat little rows by type and size. Them ready-prepared notices she does, all cardboard and sticky-backed plastic, proclaimed the special offers: though there wasn't a B.O.G.O.F to be seen, it being too common an expression for Madam's sensibilities. Even her float was compartmentalised, in a tidy little red cash box which was neatly padlocked to a sturdy canopy strut. When I turned up at twenty to, those Preserves (Preserves my arsenal; they're nothing but glorified jam.), well, they sat there mocking me, proud in their stupid frilly caps. Somebody tell me, what *is* the point of those? They just get in the way of the lid. I dumped the books onto the table, fumbled in me trouser pocket for the float – which wasn't there 'cos I'd forgotten it – and had to ask her to change a tenner for me first customer. She did that, then handed over a cup of tea which she'd made whilst I was setting up. Strong, white, two sugars.

She'd remembered.

She would.

Then, when I asked her to mind the stall for me so I could buy some late spuds for the allotment, she neatly arranged the books according to reading age while I was gone (pre-school, junior, teen, adult), with the "unsavoury" titles (her word) tucked discreetly in a box by the side of my – *my* – stall.

By the time we got to planning the Twinning Association sponsored walk, I was at the point where every single thing she said or did needled me.

The funny thing is, it started off all right. When we set out together to work out the route, we found ourselves ambling around all friendly like, as if we'd been taking Sunday afternoon rambles together for years. We chatted away like old pals, to the point where I forgot myself once or twice and had to apologise for me language. I got a bit narked when she kept jotting the route down in her notebook, but she wasn't to know how good my memory is, after all. Anyway, we got back, showed the route to the committee, and it was decided that as we were familiar with it, we should be the ones to put up signs in English and French so that none of the Twin Towners would get lost in the woods. I was quite happy to do that with her. I thought she could make the signs, whilst I would tack them to the trees. She being a woman, well, she might hit her thumb or something, and it would be a shame to spoil them pretty nails. I like nice nails on a woman.

That was my plan, anyway: but I'd reckoned without Madam. She had decided for some reason that we would start at opposite ends of the walk and meet in the middle. The signs had to be put up on the morning of the walk itself, and it was, she said, the most economic use of time. That's the way she talks. "Most economic," like she's swallowed a dictionary or something. Anyway, she explained that that's what had been decided at the meeting, but I don't remember hearing it. Them meetings always send me to sleep, anyhow. She offered to go back and make my share of signs, but I wasn't having that. I always do my bit; no-one can say I don't. I wasn't best pleased with her at that point. Just as well we didn't have to walk it together. I work better alone anyway. I dashed off my share of the signs in half an hour, with spelling and everything. I'm nothing if not efficient.

To give her her due, when it all went belly-up, she didn't try to duck the blame. I mean, a woman like her, she must find it difficult to admit to mistakes. We rounded up all the Frenchies eventually, and they were quite happy once we'd dried them off and fed them with local cheese and cider. It was obvious she'd missed out one of the signs, though I didn't accuse her, just dropped a gentle hint, like. She gave me a peculiar look – I couldn't tell if it was embarrassment or what – bit her lip, and then admitted it must have been her. It was her eyes that got me, though. They looked like… sort of like broken windows, if you know what I mean.

She got so much stick that she quietly resigned from the committee. I thought that was a bit much myself. I felt right sorry for her after all she's done. Then, when I was taking the dog for a walk, I found the sign that had blown away. Funnily enough, it wasn't one of those sticky-backed plastic creations like the rest. It could almost have been one of my last-minute efforts, if that were possible. That's why I took her that box of fancy chocolates, just to let her know I appreciate her work, if no-one else does.

When she answered the door, I could see she'd been crying, and, well, the chocolates seemed to bring it on worse. I didn't know what to do, so I started to pat her shoulder in a friendly way: and before I knew what was happening, I was kissing her. I couldn't help it, she just looked so sort of vulnerable.

48

Like I say, I never liked her, so I don't understand why I'm walking this walk in the Church with the whole village looking on. It's embarrassing, really, except that, well, she does look sort of radiant. Her eyes aren't broken windows anymore.

And she does have really nice nails.

Great Expectations

"Is this seat taken?" asked the quietly spoken stranger. Hastily, Veronica pulled the empty seat towards her.

"I'm afraid so," she said, more sharply than she intended. "I'm waiting for someone."

Unfazed by her apparent hostility, the man nodded and smiled. "Sorry I disturbed you. I'll find another."

Veronica exhaled as he went away, relieved. She watched him walk, relaxed and confident, across the familiar crowded café, threading through the tightly nested tables with minimal fuss. A nod here, a smile there and he was able to pass without trouble, his coffee held steadily in his right hand, the title of the book that was tucked under his left arm still clearly visible: Great Expectations. He had such an air of gentle, solid calm about him, Veronica almost felt a pang of regret. She watched him covertly as he approached the only other vacant spot, opposite a woman who was absorbed in her paper. Like most clients, she was a regular; Veronica recognised her face. After a moment's polite interchange the woman returned to her paper and he sat down.

It was a small snapshot in her ordered day, but it disturbed Veronica beyond the bounds of its apparent triviality. She dipped her head and sipped her Earl Grey tea, but in spite of herself she kept finding her attention wandering across the room to where he had settled. She could see him in profile quite clearly; dark hair that was silvering at the edges, strong features, steady hands. He looked kind. As she watched, she could see the woman opposite him begin to take notice, her eyes flicking over the top of her paper. Eventually she lowered it, leaned forward and made some smiling comment to him. As he responded, Veronica was surprised at the reaction it caused within her.

Was it jealousy? Impossible! She was a mature woman, not a giddy girl. At that moment, the man turned, almost as if he could read her mind, and looked at her steadily. He smiled gently, almost wistfully, she thought, as he caught her eye. Embarrassed at being caught staring she turned her attention to her tea and busied herself with pouring another cup.

Earl Grey was her favourite drink, and though it had taken a whole year to break that particular barrier, it was now her habit to come to this coffee shop once a week. The first time had been like climbing a mountain. Breathless and shaking she had only stayed ten minutes, leaving the steaming cup of tea on the table. She had run home, regardless of how ridiculous she must look, a woman of her age in stilettos and pencil skirt running full pelt, and had slammed the door behind her, grabbed the phone as if it were a lifeline, and jammed her back to the wall as her knees buckled beneath her. Her sister Jessica, her best and only friend, came round immediately like she used to before, an encouraging word on her lips, a hug of comfort freely given. That was the first time. Now of course, she was able to come here on a regular basis, and she always ordered one pot of tea with extra hot water and a chocolate brownie.

Veronica thought back to the conversation that had finally driven her out of doors.

"What is it this time?"

The sharpness of the question had caught her by surprise. Jessica never snapped.

"There was a noise out the back," she said.

Jess went to the back door and heaved it open.

"Look," she said. "There. Nothing. No-one. There are noises, Veronica. There are people going about their lives who never give a thought to you. They have lives to live that don't include anything about you. I have a life, too! Have you thought of that? Have you thought what happens in my house when you call me at six o'clock demanding attention? I'll tell you what happens; I have to leave the kids to their own devices; I have to switch off the cooker with the supper half done; I have to go and ask Sue to keep an eye out whilst I run over here to pet you and make you feel better. James comes in and his dinner's not ready and by the time I get back he's finished cooking it himself, tired as he is. It's not fair. I can't do it anymore, Veronica, I just can't. My marriage is suffering, my family – my kids need me. I know you've needed me too, but my kids need me more. They can't do anything anymore; they even had to give up Brownies because more often than not I can't take them because you need me here! Is that how you want my life to be?"

No tears came, but Veronica's throat felt dry and tight. She was stunned at the pent-up emotion that was pouring from her unflappable sister.

"I'm sorry," she managed to croak out. "I didn't think…"

Jess sighed. "No. I know you didn't think. I know you have good reason for the way you are. But sweetheart, why are you allowing one stupid, selfish idiot to rob you of your life? Look at you! Where's my sister? Where's my lovely Ronnie who was the sharpest dresser of us all, who was the life and soul of the party? You used to have friends round for coffee and girls' nights in, but now you spend all your time slobbing around in shapeless trackies, and your only entertainment is that stupid computer! You spend far too much time chatting with people you're never going to meet. It isn't helping you, Veronica. Now, I'm sorry I snapped, but I mean it. I can't do this anymore. You have to get help. Women do recover and live a fairly normal life, you know, but they have help. Some of them were really raped, Ronnie, and at least that didn't happen to you. At least you got away. He may not have succeeded in raping your body, but you're letting him rape your mind, you're allowing him to steal the life you should have. Now, think about what I've said; and here, take this card. Mary's a good friend of mine and she's a trained counsellor. She'd love to help you."

Jess went towards the door, then turned back and hugged her sister hard.

"I want to help you too," she said fiercely, "and this is the only way I know how to do it."

Veronica didn't use the card immediately. First she took the full length mirror from the loft where she had hidden it, and leaning it against the door, she dared herself to look. What she saw there frightened her. It was a thin brown mouse of a woman, whose shapeless, frumpy clothes and masculine footwear could have been deliberately chosen to hide any evidence of femininity. The hair was long, lank and undefined, covering a pallid face that didn't have a shred of makeup. Was this what they saw when she ventured out to work every day? Veronica wasn't surprised no-one took much notice of her. Every pore of her unhealthy skin seemed to send out the message "don't see me, I'm invisible." Suddenly as she looked, Veronica felt a tiny surge of indignation begin to rise. Jess was right. She was letting herself be robbed. Standing there, surveying the ruins of who she had been, she came to a decision.

Sending up a silent prayer for courage, she went to the computer and started shopping for some new clothes and make-up. The day they were delivered, she was absolutely terrified, but that little nugget of strength, born of indignation, was still sitting there in her gut, and it was beginning to grow. It took a long time for her to wear the slim skirt and red stilettos anywhere other than indoors; but eventually she got used to the smart, feminine way she felt when she wore them: and she began to like that person a lot more than the one that was cowering inside. The day she decided her goal was to wear them to work, was the day she picked up Mary's card. She was going to need help.

Veronica had finished her tea, but she still sat at the table with the empty chair pulled up next to her. She walked up to the counter and ordered another. The barista looked at her in surprise.

"You're thirsty today," she said. "I don't think I've ever known you have a second pot."

"No, I don't usually," she replied, "but I'm waiting for someone."

No need for the Barista to know the someone had already arrived. Ronnie took the tea back over to her seat, positioning herself so that she could see the quiet man quite clearly. The woman with the paper had given up trying to chat to him, finished her drink and left; he had ordered another and was sitting with his book unopened on the table in front of him, scanning the emptying café with a vaguely disappointed air, studying each table. Ronnie felt courage rising within her like a rod of steel. Her sister Jessica was sitting at the next table – when she'd heard that Ronnie was planning to meet up with an internet friend, she'd insisted on being there to stand guard – and the dwindling numbers of regular customers were unthreatening. Casting one glance at her sister, who nodded encouragingly, she got up, fished out the copy of Great Expectations that they'd each agreed to carry and took her tea over to his table. Smiling tremulously, hands shaking, she laid the book down beside his.

"Is this seat taken?" she asked.

The Romantic History of Miss Hetty Bates

A whimsical monologue attributed to a character from Jane Austen's "Emma"

It is a sad truth that no woman really understands the nature of the man she marries until after the deed is done. Indeed, I begin to wonder if in some respects I am among the most fortunate of women, although my single state was, for many years, accepted by myself and my late Mama with gentle resignation. I know Papa thought it deplorable, indeed he said as much on more than one occasion – albeit not due to any real fault of my own, unless it be in those faults common to women in the general way of things, of course. That is to say, though never a beauty, I did not count myself as a pariah among females. I would have made a good wife – or as the vicar's lady would say a good bargain... (I would not use such a term myself, of course, it is so very—) ...a good bargain for one dear gentleman had my circumstances not prevented me from entering into that much longed-for state.

To be sure, I do occasionally find myself wondering if the vicar's wife – Mrs Elton you know – if her upbringing was quite – her expressions are not, perhaps, what would have been acceptable to dear Papa. Where was I? Oh yes. I was pondering on poor dear Jane's fate. No-one could ask for a better niece, indeed, or more attentive when it comes to writing letters: but it is now six years since her marriage to Mr. Churchill and not a single visit have we had, not even when the – when she announced – when the happy event that is a natural consequence of marriage was made known to the world. Indeed, Mama and I would not even have had a sight of the child were it not for the kind efforts of my dear, dear friend Mrs Knightley, Miss Emma Woodhouse as was, and her husband. Indeed, he seems to be the exception to the rule concerning the matter of husbands, always so very attentive to Mrs Knightley and her friends.

It was his efforts, I find, that enabled us to visit the Churchills two Christmases ago, when they themselves were travelling into Yorkshire. He made the kind offer to convey myself and Mama – before she died, of course, well, naturally it wouldn't be seemly otherwise – and sent the necessary letters confirming that we were able to come. For a while, indeed, there was some doubt as to whether they would be there to receive us, Mr Churchill having one of those sudden whims that gentlemen seem to entertain so frequently. At least in my experience they do. It seemed he was wishing to take Jane and the child to a house in Bath for the winter, which would of course have been impossible for us to visit as, he said, hired houses make for such a squeeze with visitors.

However, it all fell through at the last minute – or perhaps Mr Knightley persuaded Jane that her health would not benefit, I forget – anyway, it all turned out perfectly for myself and Mama and we had a wonderful time with little Frank... I hardly dare say with Mr and Mrs Churchill, not that we had a bad time to be sure, it was rather a case of too little time with them to make any judgment in the case, which is perhaps a pity when you consider – Not that I could have done anything to prevent Mr Churchill from doing the things that it seems many gentlemen do, even the married ones as pleasant as Mr Churchill; but at least I would have been there to be a solace to poor Jane whilst her husband went about behaving in an unseemly fashion with Mrs W-. But it seemed for a while that it was all forgot, enough for there to be a second happy announcement recently, which I know gave poor Jane great joy until Mr Churchill acquired a taste for the gaming tables. I am happy that Mama did not live long enough to see it.

You may suppose it is not proper for a single lady like myself to know about such things, but you see my poor dear Papa had a sad predilection himself, fed by the temptations of the offering plate and the communion wine, which indeed caused a good deal of suffering for poor Mama and was the reason for our removal from the Vicarage to what is now our current home which, although above a shop, was originally owned by Lord H-; and indeed, it was very kind of him to make the apartment over to us when my Father had of necessity placed the living back within his disposal. I did not look for such kindness from him as no one could doubt he had no obligation to continue to house us after Papa's sad accident with the shotgun, which carried him off so precipitately. So you see it is perhaps not surprising that I have a little worldly wisdom about such things. I do hope that Mr Churchill does not turn out to be like dear Papa: that would be too, too dreadful for poor dear Jane after all her hopes.

It was in the course of writing to dear Jane that I discovered that some of my own romantic history had got about the village. It happened that Miss Woodhouse, or rather Mrs Knightley, came on a visit whilst I was penning a letter to her. To Jane I mean. I had only got to five pages – I don't know how it is but there is always so much to say to Jane – and I really was not disposed to be interrupted, but I am so grateful for Mrs Knightley's kindness in continuing her visits that I could not turn her away. Such a dear old friend. She had come with young Mrs Martin, Harriet Smith as was, and they had brought their dear little girls with them. It seems that they were a little concerned about me staying in the cottage alone so soon after Mama's demise, and had come up with a scheme (Emma, Mrs Knightley I should say, pronounced it a capital plan) little knowing the pain they were causing by their good-hearted efforts, to have me remove for a while to stay with Emma, Mr Knightley and Mr Woodhouse at Hartfield. My protests went all unheeded, and indeed it is like dear Emma's kind heart to be always thinking of others, but I dare wish in some ways she would not be quite so strong in her ideas. She is so very like her Mama: though in spite of the circumstances, Mrs Woodhouse and I did become very dear friends. Of course, any intercourse between the two houses would have been impossible had my history been generally known, but happily I had only mentioned it to Mrs Cox, she then being Miss Dorrington before she made what was considered a rather unwise choice of husband; though no-one can doubt that, although he is in trade, they deal very well together; and I am sure that she would not have mentioned it to anyone. Or nobody of consequence at least. Although I believe she did say once that the village was in sympathy with me; and when I asked what she meant, she merely turned her eyes to heaven and said, "Oh! Did I say with you? I meant with your Mother and her changed circumstances, of course!" which was much more likely. So it came about that Mrs Woodhouse and I were friends, and I'm sure she never knew that her husband had all but promised himself to me shortly before he met her. Indeed I could bear no grudge against such a lively, generous creature, and of course once we were turned out of the Vicarage I could not keep my dear Mr Woodhouse to any promise – not that a firm offer was ever made, but he had intimated that he thought he and I should be very comfortable together, and that my care for his health which was even then rather poor, had gone some way to winning his heart. It would have been so very-. For he was not exactly a young man even then; and it had been the dearest wish of my heart for some years to give him what care I could. Of course after Papa it was quite impossible. Not only had I Mama to care for, as her health was quite broken down with the worry of it all, but I could not expect Mr Woodhouse to wish to ally himself with someone in such reduced circumstances: though indeed he would have done had his Papa, old Mr Woodhouse, not told him he would not like it. I shall never forget his gentle sigh as he told me. I remember his very words:

"My dear Miss Bates, it would not be wise for us to be anything more than friends. My Father tells me I should not be comfortable. It would be a great change, a very great change indeed. I am sure I am not up to it. My health is somewhat delicate, you know, and the robustness of married life should not suit me at all."

Although of course it was very shortly after that he met Emma's Mama and discovered it would suit him after all. My solace in my sorrow, for indeed I was very fond of Mr Woodhouse, very fond indeed, my only solace was the awareness that my own conduct to him was above reproach, and that the village could know nothing about the matter. Indeed, many people continued to treat me exactly as before, only the tradesmen being a little more pressing about the money. I was so pleased. It would have been too humiliating to be the subject of gossip, and people are so swift to judge on the matter of being jilted. It is partly why I have always been so attached to my dear friend Emma: in my sillier moments I have considered that had I married as I wished, she would have been my own child. Dear Emma, she is so easy to love.

So with all this to consider you may imagine with what strength I protested against this idea, so kindly meant, of removing to stay at Hartfield, even for so short a time as a month. A stay leads to so much more intimacy than a mere supper party. It would have occasioned such deep embarrassment upon my part, such thoughts of what might have been, that I could not have borne it. Emma and Mrs Martin went away full of the idea in spite of all my efforts, and I had almost resigned myself to the prospect, when most fortunately, I was released from the obligation. The very next day Mr and Mrs Knightley called on me together. The expression on Mr Knightley's face was decidedly serious. I had almost said angry: and my dear Miss Woodhouse, Mrs Knightley I should say, was quite red about the cheeks, although upon my expressing my concern she did mention the breeze was quite stiff outside, and the fire a little too hot within.

However, before I could damp it down, Mr Knightley said, quite sternly, "Miss Bates, my wife has something she wishes to say to you, if you will do her the honour to listen for a moment."

So saying he removed the coal shovel from my hand and looked piercingly at my friend. I am quite, quite sure her lip quivered for a moment: but she held up her head, and calmly and sincerely begged my pardon for having given me pain.

"It is not the first time I have been guilty of hurting you deeply, Miss Bates, and I know it was wrong of me. My meddlesome ways have got the better of me once again, but please believe that it was done in ignorance of the history between you and my Father."

I was speechless with surprise. I looked to Mr Knightley, wondering how long he had known, for surely it could only be he that had told her of it.

He put the shovel down and gently took my hand, encouraging me to sit. "The truth of the matter is, Miss Bates, that knowing how I long for my family to be settled at my own home, Donwell, my dear wife and her impressionable young friend Harriet Martin persuaded themselves into a plan that would be most convenient to us, without any consideration of your feelings. Emma's excuse (it is a very poor one) is that the care of our daughter has naturally made her less available to the notice required by her Father. They felt that in bringing you and Mr Woodhouse together, a romance might have been kindled that would lead to Emma's duty as a daughter being superfluous. After all, a daughter can only be a burden where there is a second wife."

I wanted to speak, but although I opened my mouth, I am sure that the words did not come out.

"The only mitigation I can claim for my wife..." here he looked angrily at poor dear Emma, "...is that she was ignorant of the past history between yourself and Mr Woodhouse. I hope it is some compensation to you that the gossip about it has been so completely forgotten. Highbury does indeed have a very short memory, and your warm heart and good breeding have made people forget any nonsense that might once have sprung from your misfortune."

He shook hands with me.

"I know that you will forgive Emma: she does mean well. I bid you good day."

He raised his eyebrows at Emma, who drew near and shook hands as well.

"My behaviour has shocked you," she said. "You cannot speak. But I do hope, Miss Bates, that this will not prevent you from being a welcome visitor to Hartfield. Indeed, we had hoped you would come for a meal with us this very evening. If you can forgive me, we shall have a small party; the Westons are coming, and we shall all be comfortable together."

I think I nodded: at any rate, the Knightleys left. But indeed, if husbands can make one as uncomfortable as Mr Knightley made poor Emma, and Mr Churchill has made poor dear Jane though to a greater extent of course, I wonder that every woman does not remain single.

Poor dear Mr Woodhouse. To be sure, if he remembers me with any fondness at all, it would no doubt be most convenient – most convenient indeed.

Speaking Martin

I liked her mouth. Her lips were plump and red with some kind of gloss, like the membrane of a pomegranate seed. Dark. Translucent. She ate neatly, her lips moving so slowly, I had to keep watching. She ate with intensity, taking all the taste from each mouthful. The lips enfolded the forkful of salad, the soft, warm goat's cheese and juice of the ripe pear mingling, oozing from the corner, sliding down the little crease that was there. She didn't use her napkin. She wiped the warm stickiness daintily with her third finger, licking it with the very tip of her tongue. I approached the table and sat down.

"I like you," I said. "Can I cook for you?"

The mouth formed an O of surprise, then eased into a curve.

"That's a very direct approach," she said. White teeth peeped out as the lips embraced the words. "I don't know. Are you asking me back to yours? That's a little forward, don't you think?"

I didn't know what she meant.

"Not mine," I said, "my Mum's. The house is hers. I just live there."

The mouth pursed slightly. It made me think of a ripe raspberry. She didn't speak for a few moments.

"Well," she said, "if it's your Mum's and not yours, hadn't you better ask her first?"

I nodded, and we went to find Mum.

She came to lunch. I made a light, creamy parsnip soup, gently spiced with coriander, turmeric and cumin, with cream swirled on top. The mouth was paler that day, more polite: lamb steak done to medium without a hint of undercooking.

"I like it just pink, sometimes," I said.

Her top teeth came out and caught the bottom lip. "Do you? I didn't think you could get pink parsnips. Can you?"

"Not the parsnips," I said, "the lamb steak."

"Oh, I see," she said; but the mouth didn't embrace the words, it skipped politely over them, hardly touching. She didn't see at all.

Martin would never be able to tell you what colour my eyes are. I don't think he's raised his gaze from my mouth once in all the time I've known him. People say he doesn't communicate well, and because of that his mother Juliet goes pretty much everywhere with him. He's not aggressive; he just doesn't know how to wrap things up in a polite parcel. I told him that once. The next day he served me the most beautiful little parcels of baby spinach and feta, laced with a touch of nutmeg, lightly held in filo as crisp and winsome as an angel's wing. Simple, effective and very polite; small enough to be eaten in one mouthful, so I didn't get filo pastry everywhere. I wondered at the dexterity hidden in those fingers; so long, strong and slender. Delicious.

The evening he barged up to me and sat down, I was having what I told myself was a quiet celebratory dinner; but truthfully I was lonely. Even so, I don't know what made me say I would go and eat with him. I think it was Juliet's eyes that persuaded me. They looked dead, as if all their hope had been properly mourned long ago, cremated on the fiery tongues of the uncaring. I didn't want to be in any way responsible for that look. The instant I agreed I regretted it. Maybe I was opening myself up to more ridicule.

The soup went a long way towards assuaging my fears. Light, delicate and creamy, with a slight shock of exotic spice to stop it from sliding into mediocrity, it was hard to believe

64

that those thuggish, hefty roots that were the ballast of a million Sunday roasts could be transformed into a thing of such refined beauty. Sadly it was wasted at the time. I didn't understand what Martin was trying to say to me, so the wonder of that exquisite compliment went right over my head.

At first, Juliet would be there with us, a lean mastiff standing guard. She and I were hop-laden beer and fine wine; we didn't really hit it off. She was my death's head on a mopstick: it was impossible to look at her and enjoy eating. I've never met anyone who had such indifference to food. She would sit in martyrlike endurance whilst Martin moved deftly about her kitchen producing something Michelin-worthy. When he served it, so aesthetically glorious, she would take her fork and poke it around the dish for a while, then smile in a tired way and remark that she wasn't very hungry. She was ramrod thin, and had a will of iron. For sleep, she napped during back-to-back cookery shows. Repeats of Nigella followed by Masterchef were her idea of heaven; Martin doesn't seem to need much sleep and is only still when he's watching TV.

Mouths are interesting things. I like to watch them. Not my Mum's though; her mouth isn't interesting. It's two thin straight lines that droop slightly at the corners. It's very pale, sometimes almost blue. Not blue like steak, blue like fish. Mum hardly eats at all, except on Wednesdays when Vera comes over to watch cookery shows. She's not very hungry most days, and especially not hungry on Wednesdays, not until she goes out. I know she gets hungry then because she comes back smelling of the chippy. Her lips always look moist; it's the grease. I told her that chip fat is bad for the heart, but she clamped her lips together until there was one thin line, and said she never ate chips. I don't know why she said that. I could smell them.

65

Vera's lips are orange. I don't know what they're like underneath, I've never seen them without their orange. She makes me think of orange all the time. Once, I made her caramelised oranges to eat, and she said thank you and ate some. Even with the juice and the caramel, the orange didn't come off. I didn't spin the sugar for her, though. That wouldn't be right.

I only started to sense there might be a subtext the day he served venison steak with tayberries. He'd marinated the meat for three days – Juliet complained about the smell. He pan fried it in oil and butter and served it to me on a bed of dark, buttered greens. Dribbles of jus fingered their way lightly across the flesh, shining with oil, dripping down, surrounding it so it was marooned in a rich dark pool. Then on the top he'd laid a single, perfect, fresh tayberry, its open mouth turned towards me like a kiss. I picked it up with my fingers and put it gently between my lips. My tongue found the cavity, and the little mounds of flesh melted around it, releasing their soft, sharp juices.

She used to come for lunch twice a week. Then I said it would be better if she came for dinner instead. I told her to come on Wednesday, and Mum could tell Vera to stay home. She smiled and dipped her head so I couldn't see her mouth; but there was red everywhere. Her cheeks were redder than her lips. So I bought Moro oranges, red as blood. I pared them and sliced them, and mixed the juice and zest with the caramel, so everything was suffused with blush. Then I laid them on a rectangular platter. I mixed warmed lemon curd with rich Greek yoghurt and cream and put it at one end of the platter in a slim glass dish. It looked like a pillow. I spun the caramel. I spun it and spun it, and it was like a fine curtain draped over the dish, corner to corner, edge to edge. She didn't eat it for a long time. I thought the sugar might dissolve.

"Don't you want it?" I asked.

She made this funny snuffing noise. Her bottom lip was trembling like a soufflé, and there were runnels of wet dripping down past the corners of her mouth and into the folds under her chin, then down onto the table. This meant she was crying. I was a bit surprised, because I thought she'd really like it.

"I'm sorry," I said, "I didn't mean to make you cry. Mum says I shouldn't make people upset. I thought you'd like it."

She cried out then, really loud.

"Oh! Martin! Martin, I love it! It's just that..." Suddenly her mouth wasn't wobbling, it was laughing, and her whole body was wobbling instead. It was confusing. "...no-one has ever done anything so beautiful for me before."

"Then why did you cry?"

She said the oddest thing, but the lips were embracing the words. Lips and words were entwined together, so I knew she was telling the truth.

"I'm not crying because I don't like it. I'm crying because I do."

Those oranges were exquisite. Bitter-sweet, like the way I felt about him. Bitter, because he would never look me in the eye; sweet, because I felt like I was important to him, that I knew him with abiding intimacy. Bitter oranges, red as love, sweet romantic caramel, velvet lemon cream rolling like a warm duvet over my tongue, presented on a bed that could grace the boudoir of a harem princess. It made me feel so beautiful. That was the day I fully understood Martin's language. Juliet said he couldn't communicate; but it was just that Juliet didn't speak Martin.

We met regularly over the next six months. His skill in the kitchen was unsurpassed, and when I ate the food he had prepared so thoughtfully, his eyes watched my lips as if they were his only source of joy. Juliet left us to it. It was good for her. She started to relax about things.

This idyll had to break at some point I suppose, and it did. He simply didn't understand when I told him I had to go on a diet. I knew I'd really offended him when he made partridge wrapped in smoked bacon, loaded with garlic and ginger. The flavours argued in my mouth, then escalated to a war in my stomach. He couldn't ruin a dish on purpose, he wouldn't know how.

When I came round the following week, Juliet was there, and there was a semi-consumed shop-bought pizza on the table. Juliet looked up in surprise when I came in.

"He told me you weren't coming anymore," she said, her mouth shutting like a trap.

I turned to him.

"Is that what you want?" I asked.

He looked at my mouth.

"Is that what you want?" he echoed.

I shook my head.

"No. No, it's not what I want at all. Martin, I really love – I love coming here. I love eating with you. I don't want to stop…"

His eyes didn't leave my lips.

"…but you need to understand that the doctor says I will be ill if I don't lose weight. It's bad for my heart for me to be so big."

Eating his wonderful creations – often three courses of them – had sent me up two more dress sizes when it was already difficult to find clothes to fit me; and recently I'd been wheezing at the slightest exertion.

"Like chip fat?" he said.

I looked at Juliet, puzzled. She looked at the floor.

"I told my Mum chip fat is bad for her heart."

I sighed with relief. "Yes. Like chip fat. Martin, can I give you my diet sheet? I can still eat with you, but I have to eat smaller portions and less fat. Could you make meals like that for me?"

"Yes, of course. I can make any meals. Any meals you like."

Juliet looked up at me. Gratitude flitted across her face, lighting it for a moment, then swiftly shut down again. The jailbird could taste freedom once more, at least for two nights a week.

I knew what to do next. I took her diet sheet and I made a meal from the ingredients on it. I beat a skinless chicken breast thin and rolled it around slivers of smoked cheese, a few raisins and pine nuts, and lots of parsley. I slicked the pan with just a brush of basil oil and seared the stuffed chicken; then I poached it in a little white wine. I made a tomato and olive salad with fresh basil torn up and scattered over. Then I baked a miniature saffron teabread. I added lots of saffron and studded it with amber apricots and vibrant red cherries. They looked like jewels. I baked it in a mini Savarin mould, and it came out just right: a rich, light golden circlet, alive with colour. I set it on a red plate and put it in front of her.

Her lips pursed. I like that a lot.

"It's not for eating," I said.

"Saffron?" she asked, her lips entwining with the words.

"Ounce for ounce more expensive than gold," I said.

The lips parted, embracing the words. "Yes, Martin, I will."

Ladies Nodding Graciously

It was Dad that first tried to sell it to me, though it didn't occur to me to question under what circumstances it would be used. How could I? The introduction to the whole idea was when I was far too young to think about things like that. I just accepted it, the way I accepted everything else about him. How old was I? Let me see... old enough to remember clearly, that's certain. Not that it really matters now. I don't know why I'm thinking about it, except that it's grey all around.

I wish I hadn't come.

The images are all jumbled anyway. Spotted and washed out, they jump from the Rock of Gibraltar to the garden of our council house, and back again without notice. There's me in that frilly yellow frock and cardigan that didn't quite match, making ring-a-roses round some girl, once no doubt my friend, now only a face I don't recognise. There's my cousin, hiding in the long grass, waiting to jump out and frighten me... It's all washed in that strange tint that is more than Sepia but less than Technicolour; or perhaps it was merely monochrome, and it's my memory that has added the different shades.

There's one scene that even my memory can't colour, though. I can see it now, flickering in front of me in shades of grey. In that darkened room, grey was the only light; and no matter if the rest of it was in colour or not, that one scene was always grey, and always will be, long after I'm gone.

It's *so* cold up here.

I don't suppose for an instant Dad knew what he was doing, spilling out all that risky enthusiasm.

"I've got a treat for you," he said, as he set up the strange machine. "Sit quiet, now."

Daddy wasn't home often, but he always brought treats. Yes, I must have been very young; for child that I was, I quickly grew bored with this promised treat that was no treat at all for me. I was at the age when treats were always cellophane-wrapped – but Daddy was home, and anything he did was special.

I sat there without complaining as the Rock of Gibraltar – wrapped in disappointing celluloid – loomed strange, dark and forbidding on our familiar living room wall, closely followed by distant images of Singapore that meant nothing to me, except that Daddy had walked there. It was muddled with tales of wild monkeys walking free, and the faces of strangers laughing out at me, silent, impotent, part of his other life: his life in strange lands.

I was becoming restless. It was then, as I was wriggling to get down, that he became aware of me; and that was the moment – the moment that he tried to sell it to me.

"Just watch this next bit, pet. It's really exciting. You'll love it – you won't see anything like this anywhere else."

Caught, I sat still, curious to see what could be so exciting. The big grey wheel tack-tacked busily behind me, rotating slowly, steadily spitting out pictures; while a mere hand's breadth away its little mate picked them up, coiling them neatly inside itself.

I watch our living-room wall, prepared to be thrilled.

First of all, there's just the sea, the grey sea, moving, heaving, rising like a beast whose breath is coming all uneven. As I watch it surging, swaying, surging, swaying, suddenly it's as if I'm inside it. I start to move with it, until I nearly fall off my high stool. I'm impressed with its restlessness, but I disapprove of its greyness, so that I can't decide if I like it or not; but I feel the pull of its attraction inside my belly. For a moment it's all there is, and I wonder if that is the peak of the promised excitement.

71

Tck tck tck tck tck goes the wheel.

Now there are ships: two of them, grey, light grey, with dark letters and numbers on their sides, Naval vessels dancing strangely out of sync, moving, heaving, rising and falling, first the one, then the other, like two sedate old ladies nodding their heads graciously as they meet on their way. It looks like there is only a hand's breadth between them.

For a moment I am disappointed; but then a black speck appears between the two ships, flying wingless above the monstrous sea. The ships dance their stately dance over peak and trough, bobbing and bowing and veering to and fro without reference to each other; the black speck between them moves like a neat, busy spider swiftly from one to another.

It's getting even colder up here. It's no wonder, really; I'm wet through. My hands have gone numb, and that frightens me a little. I rub them together automatically.

I jump as the rocket is launched, its tail a lifeline and myriad prayers.

"There!" I remember him crying, excitedly, "Did you see it?"

He wound the film back again in case we'd missed it. Tck tck tck tck tck tck. There was the surging sea: there were the two ladies nodding graciously; there was the neat black spider.

There's no orchestra here, playing nobly into the night. It seems unfair until I realise that there's no screaming panic either, just a quiet, palpable sense of fear. Somewhere a woman is crying softly. People are being unnaturally polite to one another, their white faces glimmering. I become aware that I feel terribly sick; bad timing, I know, but in a way it's a comfort. It's such a plebeian thing; so ordinary. It's all I can think about for a moment, and I fool myself into thinking that soon, maybe, I'll be able to lie down.

I miss my opportunity. Someone else steps forward into the grey. I watch them apprehensively, my Father's long-forgotten excitement ringing in my head as if he were standing beside me, watching with me.

How I wish he were.

"It's a really dangerous manoeuvre," he explained as the wheels tackety-tacked on behind my head. "It's a job even to get the hawser attached from one ship to another – you got to get it right over the bows. It usually takes ooh, I dunno, quite a few attempts, but I done it first time – straight over, no messing. Rifle in me shoulder, tight in – you gotta hold it tight in, they've a helluva kick those things." He put up an imaginary weapon and aimed it in the dim room. "The kick from a gun like that could knock a man over and break his shoulder, but bouf, and over she went, taking the Coston line with her, and you should've heard the cheer! They were jumping up and down, yelling 'good shot, Tommo!' " He paused, ruffling my hair. "Your Daddy's a crack shot, girl."

He smiled at me, and I was quietly proud. I shone my love at him.

"Sometimes they use a modified Congreve Rocket, but we were mid-Atlantic on a Naval exercise, so we had the proper gun. Once you done that, and the men on the other ship have picked up the line, well, then there's the problem of actually getting across. You're trusting your life to your fellow Matlows. You can't see them on the film, 'cos I couldn't get in any closer: but there are quite a few men on the other end of the line, holding it – a bit like in a tug of war. They have to work together, paying the rope in and out with the ship as she rolls. Too loose, and you'd fall in; too tight, and the hawser could snap; and in a sea like that…" He lowered his voice dramatically, "…you'd be a goner."

73

Tck tck tck tck tck, went the wheel. Dad was in his element.

"It's a ruddy hard job for the skippers, too. They have to keep the ships as steady as possible. They wouldn't normally get that close, especially in choppy waters. They have to be very experienced to hold them the right distance apart. They could easily crash into each other."

His voice was full of importance, impressing us with the spice of dangerous living. He wound it back again. Tck tck tck tck tck. Grey sea: nodding ladies: black spider.

Before my eyes, the black spider takes on a different form; and I think I recognise it.

I can hardly breath.

"Daddy," I croak, "is that you?"

He laughs.

"That's not me, no. Who do you think was filming? But I was next across. Oh yes, I've done Breeches Buoy. That's what it's called. Can you remember that? Breeches Buoy."

I repeat the words after him in my lisping childish way, savouring them. They are unfamiliar, spiced with danger. Yes, I will remember.

I can taste the salt on my lips. It stings where I have bitten them. My hands are still numb, that's what frightens me. Won't I need to hold on tight? The sea is heaving like a breathless monster as another brave soul launches across and I watch as if it's an old memory playing itself out in the flickering monochrome of my mind. Tck tck tck tck tck, the deck beneath me creaks and cracks with the unaccustomed strain. The ships are nodding and dancing out of sync; and if the hawser snaps, they'll never get me out of there; in a sea like this, I'll be a goner.

The crewman beside me pushes me forward.

"You next ma'am," he says, his teeth flashing white in the wild grey night.

"Are you smiling?" I ask, wonderingly, as he leads me to the side of the slowly foundering vessel, enormous in her distress.

"You see ma'am," he says apologetically, "I never thought I'd ever get to do Breeches Buoy."

———————

First published by *Raw Edge* magazine.

Happily Ever After

Marlene polished the footwear methodically as she plotted the accident in her heart.

"*I could tie her bootlace across the grand staircase,*" she thought, holding up Ella's knee-high lace up boot. She visualised the plan as she rubbed in the blacking with firm, steady strokes. Ella, beautiful, graceful Ella, coming down the Grand Staircase for her Entrance on the night of the People's Charity ball, and halfway down, tripping over the bootlace stretched across from banister to wall. Head over heels. Broken leg? Broken nose? It seemed like a good idea. Halfway through her cleaning task, she laid down the blacking brush carefully and undid the bootlace from the confinement of its thirteen pairs of holes. Then she held it out at arm's length, one end in each of the skinny, work-worn fingers and thumbs. Considering its length with her thin lips pursed, she discarded the idea as impractical, and took up the boot brush again, polishing thoughtfully.

The boot finished, she took up a spangled confection with a dainty diamante heel.

I could take her dance slippers, she mused, as she held the diamante one lovingly in her hand, all sugar and spice as it was, *and polish – and polish...* she thought dreamily, *...the soles!*

A sly smile slid onto her face as she visualised Ella, beautiful, pristine Ella in her pale pink frosted ball gown with the white satin rosettes, dancing gracelessly at the Ball and trying not to slip in her shiny-as-glass shoes with the slippery-as-ice soles.

The pleasing picture popped like a bubble as Marlene put down the shoe, sighing with the unfairness of it all. Beautiful Ella would not dance gracelessly. She would never wear the slippery slippers with the polished soles. Indeed, all

Marlene's efforts in the polishing stakes were as pointless as the punishment of Sisyphus; since Ella, of necessity, always wore brand new shoes. Marlene's title, Keeper of the Royal Sandals, was an empty one. She herself knew that she was of less importance than a common bootjack.

Marlene glanced at the pile before her and picked up a single brown riding boot. *"What if I nobble her horse?"*

Upstairs in her bedroom, Ella stared at her reflection in the mirror.

"Perfection," she muttered, "perfection, oh thou elusive creature. Where art thou?"

She sighed, watching the effect in the mirror. Then she reached forward with her flawless rose-pink nail and touched the angry red spot on her reflection's lovely face. A tear welled in the corner of her cornflower blue eye; Ella watched as it rolled down her damask cheek and pondered the pathos of it all.

"How sad," she murmured. Then, suddenly, she leaned forward, staring with twitching eyes at her forehead, where the infinitesimal suggestion of a line seemed to have appeared.

"Charlene!" she screamed, horrified. "The Ultra Skin Perfection cream with Triple-Diple aromatic herbs and B.A.G's, this instant!"

Not taking her eyes off the offending crease, she took the cream handed to her without even acknowledging the ponderous girl behind.

"Oh dear, Madam," said Charlene with perfectly intoned sympathy, "surely not another wrinkle?"

"Another?" said Ella, frostily. "What do you mean another?"

"To be sure, Madam," said Charlene, her eyes lowered, "I didn't mean anything."

"You definitely said **another**," snapped Ella. "Another wrinkle in addition to…?"

Not a hint of satisfied malice showed in Charlene's impassive face. "In addition to that naughty old zit, Madam, of course."

Ella rubbed the Ultra Skin Perfection cream with Triple-Diple aromatic herbs and B.A.G's into the offending wrinkle, working away with business-like fingers.

"How many times must I tell you, Charlene? Princesses don't have zits; they have flawless damask cheeks, with perhaps the chance eruption of an Itinerant Beauty Spot. Nor do we suffer from wrinkles, merely the occasional delicate wisp of a fine line. The only exception to this is possibly the Sleeping Princess, who can legitimately claim that hers are pillow creases." She paused, considering her reflection critically. "Anyone who's slept for a hundred years and come out looking like *her* can be allowed to have a crease or two, wouldn't you agree?

"I couldn't say, Madam, I'm sure," said Charlene.

Ella started applying New Ten Cm –Thick Zit Cover (guaranteed to cover the most gruesome of zits) with expert strokes.

"I suppose I could lend her some of this," she said, squinting at the blurb on the very expensive packaging, "but the poor thing is so depressed after the loss of all her family and friends at once, I don't think she'd appreciate it properly, do you?"

"Probably not, Madam."

"Anyway," continued Ella, "when you are the only survivor of one hundred year's slumber, I don't suppose the appearance of the odd wrinkle affects you in quite the same way as it does your normal Princess. This is fairyland, after all, where anything can happen."

"…and not all of it beneficial," muttered Charlene, sotto voce.

"Pardon?"

"Just agreeing with you Madam. Of course it won't affect Princess Aurora in the same way. Oh, no, indeed, Madam," she continued, her round eyes showing not a mite of slyness. "How could it? After all, she doesn't really have to *work* at keeping her handsome prince interested, does she, all hedged in that big old castle by a thorny rose bush as he is? Poor thing. I wonder if he knew that once he got in, he would never be allowed to leave without her? It's a little bit of a different game for you and the Playboy Prince, isn't it? I mean, he could leave whenever he wanted."

"The Playboy Prince..." Ella stared, stricken, at Charlene for a moment, then hurriedly changed the subject. "Where are my buckle shoes?"

"I'm sorry Madam," said Charlene, "I can only find one."

"Again? Oh, no! Whatever will His Highness say? I suppose we'd better open another box."

Obediently, Charlene opened the large wardrobe where the new shoes were stacked twenty high by three deep.

"And take that one down to the shoe room. I'm sure the other one will turn up one day."

Then, forgetting her problems for a moment, she smiled kindly at Charlene, looking much more like the Cinder Ella the public knew and loved.

"Then, since this is going to take some time, my dear, you may take the evening off."

"Oh, thank you, Madam," said Charlene.

Down in the Shoe Room, Marlene had cleaned her way through ten boots (right foot) of varying lengths, fifteen soft leather walking shoes (ten right, five left), eight designer evening shoes (50-50, no matches) and was just starting on a small mound of kid leather practice pumps of assorted colours, with a soft rag and a dish of milk.

"Here sis," said Charlene, "another oddment."

Marlene frowned.

"What type?" she asked.

"Buckle."

"Bother," said Marlene, "I did those an hour ago."

"I don't suppose it's worth looking…?"

Marlene snorted.

"Don't tell me. 'Take it down to the shoe room,' " she mimicked. " 'I'm sure the other one will turn up one day.' I've searched these shoes till my fingers are as leathery as they are, and never found a match yet. I don't know how he lives with it, personally. It was a bad day for us – and him – when that glass slipper slipped its way on to her slimy little foot."

"Well, yes," said Charlene, "but it was quite cushy at first, wasn't it? I mean, she *was* kind to us, considering. Trying to find us husbands. Giving us nice little rides in her cucumber coach."

"Wasn't it a pumpkin?"

"No, definitely a cucumber. They tarted it up for the press release. Pumpkins are more PC."

"Well, whatever it was, I still say you're too soft. It'd take more than a few blind dates and a ride in a glorified vegetable to win *me* over."

"Oh, come on, let's be fair. Only the three mice were blind."

Marlene slopped the now tepid milk over another ballet pump. "True: but I don't count Rumpelstiltskin as a proper date; and as for the Beast…"

"Oh, don't mention *him*," moaned Charlene. "If only I'd known what lay behind that rough exterior, I could have put up with the fleas."

"Yes, and I would have taken him *without* the handsome prince bit, if only I'd known that his bank balance was as bulbous as his belly."

They sighed.

"Come on," said Charlene, "you can knock off now. Her ladyship has graciously given me the night off. She won't come and check to see if you've finished; she'll be too worried wondering whether His Nibs has fallen for the latest cover girl."

"As if he would!" Marlene chuckled. "It was a stroke of genius when you put that idea into her fluffy little head. She tortures herself with the thought that when she loses her looks, she'll have lost him, too. She knows as well as we do: this is fairyland, where anything can happen – and not all of it beneficial."

"Well," she continued, considering, "I don't know. I liked it better when she cared more for *us*. She hasn't even bought us a present recently. Spends all her money on creams and lotions for that flawless skin of hers."

"Don't worry, it definitely won't last much longer," said Marlene. "I've thought of a scheme that will put His Lordship off her for good, and when it does…" she smiled like a hungry dog. "I'll have him, and you can have Dandini."

Over in the Hall of a Hundred Mirrors, Prince Charming waited patiently for Ella.

"Oh, Dandini," he said, "you were wise not to get married. It changes them, you know."

Dandini turned to his friend, surprised. "Nonsense, PC. Ella hasn't changed a bit. I was saying so to old Mother Goose the other day. Still as flawless as the day you met her."

"Oh, looks-wise, I agree; but I'm beginning to think it was a mistake to marry a girl simply because her foot fits. It's not really much of a qualification for married life."

Dandini shrugged. "Is it the shoe problem again?"

"No, no, I'm used to that now. She's always as careless as a two-year-old with her shoes. Actually, it's one of the things about her I find endearing. I really only tackled it because Dad thinks it'll end up bankrupting the Kingdom. Personally, I think it's good for economic relations."

"Leather imports as good as ever?"

"Best they've ever been. No, I wouldn't mind living with the shoe problem if only I could have my old, sweet-natured girlie back again; but she's got so obsessive about her looks lately…"

The double doors opened as he spoke.

"The Princess Ella," announced the footman.

"Darling," said Prince Charming, stepping forward with both hands outstretched, "even these hundred mirrors aren't enough to do you justice. You look gorgeous, as ever."

He reached down to kiss her damask cheek, and then reached for his lace hanky to wipe the New Ten Cm -Thick Zit Cover (guaranteed to cover the most gruesome of zits) off his lips.

Instinctively, Ella frowned.

Immediately, a hundred Ellas frowned back at her, and the New Ten Cm -Thick Zit Cover (guaranteed to cover the most gruesome of zits) cracked across her forehead.

As she looked in horror, it cracked even more.

"Ooh," she fumed. "You… you stupid *Man*, you. Look what you've done! That's it! I won't be appearing at the ball tonight. Make my excuses!"

"But darling," cried Prince Charming, "it's the People's Charity Ball! They've all come hoping to see *you*."

"Can't be done," said Ella. "It took three hours to get this stuff on smoothly. By the time I re-do it, it'll be past midnight!" Then she and her hundred reflections turned and flounced off.

PC turned to Dandini. "See what I mean?"

"Yes," said Dandini. "Strange girl. My sister uses that stuff, you know. Perhaps you ought to explain to her that it's only meant to cover the odd zit, not your whole face."

PC shook his head. "It's more than my life's worth to mention the word zit to her. She's a martyr to her complexion. Take it from me, Dand, old chum, you did the right thing staying single."

The odds against Marlene's evil little scheme succeeding were colossal: but this was fairyland, where anything could happen, and not all of it beneficial...

The People's Charity Ball was the event of the season. Hosted by Prince Charming and the Princess Ella (known affectionately as Cinder Ella) it had been a resounding success ever since their marriage ten years before. The photojournalists were there in their hundreds, and an invitation to this prestigious event was greatly to be desired. Tonight's special guests included Princess Isadora of the Golden Ball with Prince Ferdy the Frog Prince, and of course Aurora (otherwise known as the Sleeping Beauty) and her handsome consort Florimund of the Ancient Rose Castle. Guests came from far and wide to experience the entertainment, digging deep in their pockets for the Old Crone's Benefit Fund, a charity that made decent disguises available to Old Crones across the kingdom, evil and good alike. Of course, since Snow White's little problem, they no longer supplied apples or other foodstuff, for health and safety reasons.

Tonight's ball, however, did not seem to be going quite as planned. The guests had all arrived, and had been greeted, not by Fairyland's most famous couple as they had been eagerly anticipating, but by Prince Charming's much less exciting friend Dandini; and with no other excuse than that the Princess Ella was indisposed. The paparazzi were becoming restless, and the guests were whispering among themselves, always a bad sign. Dandini started the dancing by asking a pretty, young fairy instead of a spinster princess, which put him in the bad books of all the chaperones that were present, and after the first dance Prince Ferdy made his excuses and left, leaving his wife to dance with whomever should care to ask her. Since she spent the whole evening looking daggers at all who dared approach, no-one did care, especially if you understand that in Fairyland, it's entirely possible that looking daggers can be physically dangerous.

The Princess Aurora had had a blazing row with Prince Florimund – rumour had it that it was something to do with a leak in the turret room of the Ancient Rose Castle – and had refused to turn up. Then, partway through the second waltz, Prince Charming arrived on his white horse wielding two empty champagne bottles. Nothing too unusual about that, perhaps; but instead of stabling the mare outside, he chose to ride her right through the ballroom, where she deposited a little present which, though perhaps beneficial for the roses, did nothing for the couture shoes that graced the pristine ballroom floor. Then he galloped into the banqueting hall, hoisted his steed on to the table and leaning out of the saddle, deftly swiped a full bottle of champagne.

Taking a deep draught, he cried, "My dear Princess Ella is under an evil enchantment. I go to rescue her! Onward, Prince Charming, you **shall** be victorious!"

At which point he fell out of the saddle and onto the floor, but not before he'd taken half the contents of the banqueting table with him. All in all, the only people who really enjoyed the evening were the photojournalists, who had enough coverage to keep them in ill-gotten profit for the coming year.

The result of this fracas was that Prince Charming, pleading a slight headache, did not go riding with his wife as was their custom the following day. Thus it was that Ella set out alone, with only her two step-sisters as her companions, their status as her honoured ladies in waiting making it a perfectly natural arrangement.

They returned, eyes sparkling, without her.

"Sisters, where is my dear wife?" cried the Prince, ice pack clutched to his throbbing head.

Marlene and Charlene looked at each other and composed their features into a sorrowful mask.

"So sad," said Charlene, without a hint of triumph in her voice.

"Oh, indeed," echoed Marlene, proffering a single riding boot.

Horror grew in the Prince's face.

"My wife! She's not... she's not..."

"Shoeless?" finished Marlene. "Well of course she is. Got her heel caught in the stirrup, and over the top she went, leaving one boot behind. Tragic, really. Don't worry though, PC: I'll comfort you, dear boy, and you'll soon forget her."

"But... but..." cried Prince Charming, bewildered. "Where is she?"

Charlene shrugged.

"Last time I saw her, she was sitting on a rock with a boot in her hand and a designer bag over her head. Don't worry, PC, she knows it's all over; she landed right on her pretty nose. She's quite happy to let you divorce her. She'll never be a porcelain princess again."

Prince Charming took three strides forward and clutched the sisters' hands in his.

"You darling girls!" he cried, and for the first time he kissed them both.

85

Gleefully they glanced at each other and puckered up for more, but it was too late. He was gone.

"What—"

Dandini came forward. "Well done, girls. At last you've succeeded where everyone else has failed."

Marlene looked at him mystified. "You– you mean you *wanted* us to get rid of her?"

Dandini was scandalised. "Rid of her? Of course not! It's just that nothing we said could convince her that PC loved her for her kind nature, not just her good looks. Now that she's got a broken nose, well – she won't have to keep up to impossible standards, will she? No, girls, you've done a good thing. PC and Ella can look forward to years of living happily ever after."

Marlene stuck the buckle shoe on the shoe tree.

"Soppy ending," she said, disgustedly.

Charlene sighed. "What do you expect? It is fairyland, after all, where anything can happen, and not all of it beneficial."

She paused as she espied something in the pile. "Oh look," she said, "isn't that a matching shoe?"

Previously published in the *Alternative Renditions* anthology, Bridge House publishing.

Darcy Doesn't Live Here Anymore

I don't know what made me decide to marry Darcy. I think I felt sorry for her. I mean, she was always fun, a good laugh, y'know? When the lads went out for a curry and a pint, Darcy would be there, quaffing lager and competing to see if she could get through the vindaloo before anyone else. She was always well laid back, never losing her temper or anything, and if I wanted a night out with the lads on my own, she would just smile and tell me to have a good time. I was good to her because she was so undemanding, and she seemed so grateful when I noticed her. Don't get me wrong, it wasn't that you could miss her, really, she wasn't a mouse; but she was the kind of girl that was everyone's mate, know what I mean? All the lads had a soft spot for her. Barry even told me that he was jealous; that I was a lucky sod to be marrying her – but he was drunk at the time. Everything looks good when you're pissed.

I didn't even try it on with her until after the wedding. Darcy, funnily enough, is quite old fashioned. I respected that – and respected her. I'm a good-looking sort of guy, and there were plenty of tarts out there ready to give what I wanted without strings, and I made sure Darcy never knew about them. Or if she did, she never let on. That'd be just like her. Well, anyway, I was rewarded for my self-control, and it was worth the wait; she had knockers you could get lost in. Cuddling up to Darcy was like having toasted marshmallows on a winter's night. She was all soft and warm and eager to please. I read somewhere once that fat birds try harder, and I think it might be true; though Darce was the only fat bird I ever fancied. It wasn't just that she was a good shag, either; she could cook up a storm. I've never eaten so well as when Darcy lived here. She did this amazing thing where she wrapped a piece of beef in pastry;

and then there was some Russian sounding thing, boganoff, or something, with cream. She'd cook meat with puddingy stuff, you know? Fruit, like duck with cherries, or pork with pears or apples. You wouldn't believe it would taste so chuffin' good. She loved trying new recipes. If I wanted to watch a blood & guts movie, she would curl up beside me, her hair all down like rain over her face, and her legs over my lap, and read a recipe book. You know, proper read it like she was reading a novel. She could do all that fancy foreign stuff, as well as a good old British curry or stellar fish 'n' chips in a beer batter. Whoever would have thought you'd put beer in with fish? But it worked. It was like living over a restaurant. It was a good life.

Darcy got fatter and fatter, and started going out less. She said she was quite happy for me to go; but she got embarrassed when she couldn't fit her backside on the chairs in the curry house. It was the only time I'd ever heard her mention her weight.

She got a bit down after that. She wanted babies. Well, I wasn't bothered about babies much, but if Darcy wanted one, I thought it might keep her occupied while I was at work. It was good fun trying, too; she'd been getting a bit coy in the bedroom because of her bulk; but the idea of trying for a baby seemed to awaken her old enthusiasm. It didn't work though. The quack said she was too fat to conceive and needed to lose weight. I told her not to bother. She had me, didn't she? What more did she need? I married her when she was fat, and I was happy for her to stay that way. I never had to worry about other blokes trying to take Darce away from me. She wouldn't go, anyway, she loved me, I knew that; but most blokes don't fancy fat birds. I see why, but they don't know what they're missing. Darcy was always waiting for me when I came home from work. Her one aim in life was to please me. What's not to like?

Things started to change after I got turned down for the rugby team. I didn't pass the basic medical. I was gutted, and Darce started to worry about my health. I don't know what she was thinking, couldn't bear the idea of me being anything less than 100% I suppose, but she went mental. Started to fuss about diet and stuff. Well, I never noticed, but apparently she revolutionised our eating habits. I don't understand how she did it – there were baked spuds coming out of my ears, and so many vegetables on the plate there was hardly room for meat. If anything, we ate even more. My health did pick up though – I just needed a bit of rest that was all – and I got back onto the team, so eventually she started coming out for curries again, but she wouldn't eat the ones that had all that sauce crap on; she would have chicken tikka and nick a spoonful of my gravy. She'd gone all posh on the drinks front, as well, knocking back a gin and tonic and lime sodas instead of pints. Her bottom fit fine on the chairs. I wondered why she'd ever stopped coming.

Then all of a sudden, she started going out without me. She'd go out shopping. Shopping! Stupid. What was wrong with the catalogues she used to use? Why did she need to go out into the high street to buy clothes? She came home one day all flushed and excited, dressed in these tight jeans and 3-inch heels. She started talking about the people she'd met, and about the possibility of going for a job. That's when I realised she wasn't my Darcy any more.

She wasn't my Darcy. I'd woken up one morning married to a strange woman with cheekbones you could hang your hat on.

I dumped her. Packed her bags for her and told her to go. She pleaded with me to go to one of those marriage patcher-uppers, but I wasn't going to go there to be told I was a crap husband. They're all weighted in favour of the woman, those places. I knew I was being harsh, because she wouldn't have a clue how to get on in life without me. Once she went back to being the way I liked her, I'd let her come back. I told her that, too.

I saw Darcy the other day. I hadn't seen her for a while. I don't go out much these days, see; I can't be bothered. She was still quite slim but was dressed in a smart skirt and low heels and had done something with her hair – it was all short and flicky. Quite sexy really. She was holding the hand of a pretty little girl. I stopped to talk to her. She said she was working as a chef in that posh French place in the high street. She'd won awards for a healthy nutritious cookbook she'd written. She was married again, to my old mate Barry. The little girl was their daughter.

I'm not jealous or anything, but I always knew she'd have gorgeous kids.

Rhapsody in Blue

The Liner is leaving next week; it's time to say goodbye. I can't stay, I'd be a ticking time bomb. If they discovered the truth, who knows what they'd do to me?

I love her. She's the reason I stayed here, among this weird, crazy, diverse community. I don't understand them; a lifetime wouldn't show me what they're really like. Their attention to detail is amazing; they take joy in the tiniest flower, watch a bird as it washes itself in a puddle, see pictures in clouds – can you believe that? I mean, it's just vapour, isn't it? But no, it's a face, or an animal, or food. Candyfloss, she calls it. Of course, seeing the detail has its downside. She can't stand ants in the kitchen. She gets rid of them. I disagree. Once I noticed them, I studied them. They're clever, and as a social group can achieve much, but her reaction to them is disproportionate. Knowing how I felt, she did try; but she says they're creepy, and she can't tolerate them near her food.

I don't want to leave. It's not that I've got used to her – her smell, her lovely little eyes, blue as the sky, surrounded by dark lashes that seem to emphasise their colour; her pale, glorious, curly hair that stops halfway down her back – it's more that I can't see how my life will be, without her.

We met one summer's day in the park. I'd been hit by a car – nothing serious, just a bit of a shock – and had walked there to get away. I didn't want to be carted off to a hospital to be poked at. I sat on a bench and tried to pull myself together. Physically, I was fine; but mentally I was a little shocked, and it was putting me out of kilter. She followed me to see that I was alright. She sat down beside me and looked in my eyes, taking my hand as if to take my pulse. I snatched it away.

"It's fine, I'm fine," I said, sharply.

"Are you sure?" she said, looking at me with those eyes. "You look a bit green about the gills. Would you like a glass of water? A cup of tea? For the shock?"

I looked at her, suddenly afraid, but saw nothing but kindness. No horror; no fear. I rubbed my hands; they still felt strange.

"Tea. Tea would be good," I admitted, gruffly.

As she went to a café to get the tea, I looked at my timepiece. I had an hour before the liner was due to leave; time to drink the tea, gather my wits, and get to the dock. But the accident must have had more effect than I thought; I phased-out for a while, and when I came to, I was in her house.

"How did I get here? What time is it? Have I missed my ship?"

"Don't panic. You went a bit strange for a while. Kind of passed out standing up. You walked here with me; don't you remember? You've been here… maybe an hour? You're still very green, are you feeling ok?"

"An hour! I've got to go!"

"But I've made you some more tea; and you don't look well. You had quite a knock back there. I was surprised you got up and walked away from it; you actually dented the car, you know. Do you have somewhere important to be?"

If only she knew. It was already too late. The ship couldn't wait. It had to catch the window; and it would be fifty Earth years before the next one came.

Blue Planet tea is amazing. We don't have anything like it at all. There are Gardavians who would traffic it if they could; but they'd be caught. It turns our skin pink, so you can't hide it. It was one of the reasons I wanted to visit, to try tea; I can't afford it at home.

We have shapesuits that make us appear human; it takes concentration to maintain, but it becomes second nature after a while; and even when we phase-out – we don't sleep as Blues do, we phase-out every week or so, just for one of their days – our subconscious keeps things working; we can move and speak, but we're what she would call "not all there".

I'd heard rumours of Gardies missing the ship; but I never thought I would be one of them. I had enough money to live – Blues go mad for our pebbles; Earth doesn't have many, so they're highly prized. A handful of pebbles can keep you for a lifetime; there are traders, but they're limited as to how many they can bring. Flooding the earth with what they call Diamonds would be catastrophic. Not only would they lose their value, but someone somewhere would start to wonder. They may be a simple, two-eyed, hirsute people; but they're not stupid, and it's vital they don't know who we really are. They're xenophobic; knowing about us, they'd be afraid, and fear would turn them aggressive. Fortunately, with at least fifty Blue years between trips, they can't trade tea for pebbles illegally; their lifespan isn't long enough. If it was, they would probably succeed, given their ingenuity. They're cunning; they'd adapt the shapesuit so it would hide any blushing. It wouldn't occur to a Gardavian to do that. It's their attention to detail; they may be two-eyed, but they see a lot. We see the bigger picture. No, it's best they're kept in ignorance.

That day, after drinking the amazing tea, I knew I could make it here; and I don't think she's ever suspected. Maintaining the shapesuit became second nature – they're attuned to our brain patterns and eventually become like a second skin – although she always says I look pale during phase-out. "You're off-colour today," she says. Sleep is an easy pretence: I just spend the night gazing at her. Gardies say you can't tell Blues apart: but I recognised her right from the start.

It's going to hurt to leave, but I have at least an earth lifetime and more left to live. My girl is still my girl; but her glorious hair has thinned and faded; and her beautiful creamy skin sits loosely on her bones. I know what happens to Blues; I've seen it. They stop. They have no choice in the matter. They slow down and just stop, and all that's left of them is their outer shell. Her time is coming, and I don't think I can bear to see it. But I've started to think like them, I can think from her point of view. If I leave now, then she'll be alone when she stops, and that would be terrible for her. She has no-one else.

"I love you, Agardie. You won't ever leave me, will you?" she says, sometimes. When she asks that, I know she's afraid. She hugs me close, and I snuggle my face into her, smelling her beautiful hair.

"How could I leave you, Blue? I love you too."

"Why do you call me Blue?" she asked me once.

She calls me Agardie because that day, when she walked me to her dwelling, she'd asked who I was. In my phased-out state, I'd told her I was a Gardie.

I answered her question untruthfully. I said it was because of her eyes; but I call her Blue because humans are obsessed with blue. They spend their cash chasing blue sky and sea. When their sky and sea are grey, they often feel what they call blue. Some of them go sort of blue-ish when they stop; and of course, their planet is blue. They have a song about it; Planet Earth is Blue, it says; and it's true, because sometimes, it is an unhappy planet. They're good at that – making words mean more than one thing at a time. I've come to love it.

So this is the end. Shapesuits don't last forever, and although mine's not fading yet, I don't know how long it'll last. The liner will have docked already, and I have a few days to work out how to leave.

She comes into my study.

"Agardie," she says, "it's time, isn't it? You're leaving."

I look at her.

"I've always known you would have to go. I'm lucky you've been here so long."

I am dumbfounded, afraid to speak in case I give myself away.

"I saw you. That day on the bench, when you passed out, you turned green. You really turned green, and your hands, your eyes – well – they weren't like mine; so I took you home, and I said nothing because you were so lost, and so brave, when your ship had left without you. I wanted to look after you, and I have, haven't I, Agardie? And you've looked after me, too. But now it's time to go. I'll die soon, and when I'm gone," her eyes fill with salt water, the way they do, "you'll have no-one."

I look at her, her tiny, damp, blue eyes surrounded by the hair they call lashes, fewer and paler now; her beige skin, loose but still beautiful on her bones; and I know I can't leave her. I'll stay on the blue, blue Earth, and gaze longingly up to the stars that hold my dusty home; I'll look at the vapour she calls cloud and see her face in it; and I decide that when she's gone, I will live, without regret, on the memory of my Blue. And if the ticking time bomb goes off – if my shapesuit fails and they find out what I am – I will take what comes, like a true Gardavian.

When I wake up from my next phase-out, I find I'm on the ship home. Those two-eyed Blues, they see so much; and mine is a clever little thing. I have a vague memory of her face in front of mine as she kissed me for the last time.

"Goodbye, my Agardie. Have a wonderful life."

First published by *Writing Magazine*; winner of the Other Worlds competition.

Burning Bright

The cat sat on the mat. It was a round mat, rust coloured with a pale green edge, and it complemented the cat's ginger coat. The sun, magnified, poured in through the closed window making the room feel unseasonably warm. The cat stretched luxuriously, his white paws unsheathing, graceful but unseemly like a tart's fingernails at a genteel soiree. He settled again, his yellow eyes narrowing to slits.

"Not as warm as it looks out there," remarked Patricia.

She sat in her normal seat – the one nearest the radiator – and shook out the local paper. The animal granted her a few purring breaths. The human female liked to think of him as contented. His head rested a moment on the sheathed cat paws. Pad rested over pad, firm yet soft as white cotton wool; but in the quiet lazy evening a cat dream, lit with sepia and silver, began to unfold as the sun faded.

Stalking in the moon-washed night, whiskers a-twitch, picking up the vibrations in the air like a skilled violinist. The paws glide silently like a skater, glimmering in the dark. A shiver of anticipation makes the hair stand on end for a brief, delicious moment. The cat's tiger body pauses, one paw poised in mid-air, catching the night scents zinging, tongue-tingling, like fresh ginger on the palate of a connoisseur.

He tastes the smells.

Noise there is, but secondary to scent; man's noise like white noise hissing, unless – yes, there; there it is: too high-pitched for human ears.

Yes.

He hunkers down. He knows he cannot be seen.

His prey is first unaware…

then…

dead.

He sniffs, disdainfully. His nostrils are full of vole blood. His blood-lust is sated, his edge dulled. He licks a claw, unconcerned, uninterested: then sits like an Egyptian god before the sacrifice, glassy eyed and unblinking. Time has no meaning.

Aeons later his rough-hewn tongue rasps himself into purity. This earnest cleansing is a ritual not needed, for the kill was swift and neat.

Instinct slaked, he relaxes…

…too soon. A lightening blur of fur and claws announces the criminal intent of one of his own kind. Before he can move, the yellowed teeth of his lean, wild rival snatch his own unwanted prize. Unthinkable humiliation flicks him, stinging action from his rest-lazy limbs. He is sleek, fast, invincible. Though replete, the hunter brooks no usurper. The chase will not be long. The wildcat is mean, but his need is too desperate, he cannot hold the pace, he is too easily caught. Feline screams pierce the crisp, clean air into shards once, twice, three times or more, until the watching night echoes, resounding with shrill agony. Stillness descends again. No need to ask how fares the night, for the vanquished wild foe skulks drunkenly into the void. The house-tiger holds the field, the vole held aloft in triumphant jaws, its short tail a victory pennant. He stalks proudly, daring all comers with his sparking yellow eyes. Alone his steps command the centre of Dead End Lane. Not for him the slinking ways of commoners. Not for him any hiding in the shadows. Victorious, he leaps, and firmly treads the narrow fence, confidence oozing from his sinuous limbs. Who dares come near? Who dares?

In the still night an ugly pattering and snuffling breaks his lap of honour. A footstep sounds: the skirmish may be won, but fresh battle awaits. A different enemy is roving his way, seeking to drive him under cover. Nimbly he descends to the open street, seeks a shrub for strategic concealment. Quietly he waits. This enemy requires watching. The slobbering sound creeps obscenely upon his ear, roils offensively in his guts, but still he bides. Patience. Patience. A human voice murmurs warm and deep, and with a snap the hated enemy, the dog, is off its lead. Now the time for concealment is past. He lays his prize under the shrub, saunters into the street, and prepares to stare down his ancient enemy.

The foe follows every separate scent without discrimination, unaware of his danger. The tiger-cat waits in full view, even seeming idly to tidy his froward fur, the kerb his stage, the feeble pool from the lamp his spotlight. This is a performance for a more discerning audience than the one approaching, a performance that he alone can properly appreciate. Closer and closer the mutt's nose follows its own whimsical way, darting first this way and then that, here and there until suddenly – the scent is caught: awareness strikes. The enemy's head rears: its body trembles: the bait's taken. In a flash, the cat's an arch, his fur a cockade on his ridged spine. His eyes are like searchlights on an unsuspecting victim.

"Come," he whispers, "come to me, my ancient enemy, come: see with what a swift sure strike I claw your eyes and sear the delicate tip of your tender nostrils…"

Like a foolish moth to the consuming flame the dog comes running, then as the tiger-cat spits, his claws raking like fire on the face, it turns and runs yelping, its tail lowered. The hero rests on his haunches, watching with calm satisfaction centre stage, and casually avoids the swiftly slung stone with a mere skitter. The human protector of dogs is a poor loser.

The field is won, the foe vanquished. He takes up the

vole his prize and searches, insatiable, for a new realm to conquer.

Down the alley to the corner, and the rigid asphalt river spreads before him. It gleams, still and innocuous in moonlight shimmer; but he is not deceived. Though all seems quiet, who knows but that an avenging Cerberus will come upon him, exacting its pitiless revenge, beckoning him to oblivion with its blinding, beacon eyes. Minutes tick by as he watches warily. No easy conquest awaits him here: this is the danger zone. Once or twice he challenges the road's edge with a paw, uncertain of his reception. All remains quiet. Surely this is his night of total triumph. Swiftly, nerves stretched to the zenith, he trots onto the smooth surface, aping confidence. As he nears the far edge a flattened pelt stops him in his tracks. He sniffs: the thing is mangled, unrecognisable in all but that it was once a living creature. He hesitates; it is nearly his undoing. From the abyss of night Cerberus descends with a hideous roar; and sinews bunching, he springs for safety. In a welter of noise and noxious vapour the Monster screeches once and is gone, but the wind of its passing brushes his fur as close as a lover's kiss. He looks after it in disbelief. So swift, so strong, it's a stinking, acrid alien! He has escaped its jaws, he has reached the other side, but at what cost? He is stranded now – who knows how many adventures away from safety?

He picks up the vole, his talisman, of necessity abandoned at the kerb. He rests a moment, winded, ears a-cock for hidden dangers. He, even he, does not want to take on another foe yet. A moment's respite and all has to be well; he dare not give time for his meagre courage to fail. Focused, firm-legged, he launches himself back across the brooding death-pit, looking neither right nor left. His honest bravery is rewarded by silence.

Through the long night his hard-won prize is carried with pride. Though he wants it not for himself, it is a badge of honour, ameliorating his battle scars and his near-humiliation by the asphalt river. The pallid moon wanes, her light slowly dying like a white consumptive maiden before the first flush of dawn. The dream is fading too, flickering in and out like a guttering candle; but there is time yet, time to return to a hero's welcome, time to bear his prize for the human woman, dependant on him (as he dreams she is) for her succour. She meets him, catlike, as he ascends his throne; a circle of rust-red earth, surrounded by the greensward freshened now with morning dew. As he lays his tribute at her feet, she pays him homage. But as she bows with her face to the ground, the image shifts and splits, confusing him. The rusty earth swirls with shimmering pale green, and warms and softens. His human is calling; her voice catches his ear.

"Tiggy! Tiggy darling, come for din-dins!"

The swirling earth resolves itself into a rust and green rug.

The cat lay on the mat. The sun was almost gone, leaving a trace of chill in the air. Waking slowly, he sat, not even a whisper of tiger left in his demeanour. It may have been that many adventures were awaiting him in the autumn dusk, but in the kitchen his sustenance was beckoning with seductive perfume. He followed Patricia as he always did and rubbed himself round her legs. When he becomes bored with his human slave, adventure will still be crouching outside the window; but until then he is here, and here he will find no wildcat, no ancient enemy, no roaring Cerberus to take his hard won Cattykins from him.

Remember, Remember

Rachel wasn't there this morning. Anyone looking into her watery blue eyes would have remarked the lack; it was quite obvious. Rachel wasn't really there. She was reaching inside herself for a particular something... surely it was important that she got up: surely there was something special happening today.

Her surroundings didn't bother her. The narrow bed, with the crisp, cotton sheets that chafed her old parchment skin was familiar now, and she remarked it not at all. Burgundy uniforms with people-shapes inside them marched up and down. This, too, did not alarm her as they blended into the background, part of the here and now – right, acceptable. A white uniform brought something on a tray, but Rachel waved it away, ignoring the cheery greeting, reaching again for the important something, the something that had irritatingly slipped away again.

A burgundy uniform was leading someone to her bedside. The someone didn't fit. Belonging somewhere else, it created a jarring note in the surroundings. Rachel began to feel hot. She pulled at the covers tucked tight over her legs.

"It's all right, Rachel, don't worry about getting up yet. Aren't you going to have your cup of tea, dear? Look, there's someone to see you."

Rachel wasn't worried about the sing-song voice; it fitted in with the white-sheeted bed and the burgundy uniform; but the face that leaned close to her, kissing her dry and delicate cheek with familiarity, perturbed her in a way she could not understand.

"Who is it?" she said, pettishly. "What do you want?"

Somewhere deep inside she sensed that there was something expected of her by this nameless face, and anxiety plucked at her, unrecognised. Her heart began to beat uncomfortably hard. She shoved the person, the source of her anxiety, away. The nameless face crumpled slightly, controlling its expression as best it could.

"It's me, Mum, it's Shirley. Don't you remember me?"

Shirley drove automatically to the viewpoint at the top of the hill. The handbrake squeaked as she put it on firmly, but she didn't hear it. For a few moments she sat there, unseeing. How could her mother possibly forget her? Days, months, caring for her at home, she had endured Rachel's endless repetitions, the embarrassment of night-time wanderings – endured being the outlet of her frustrations, telling herself it was all part of the illness, until, unable to bear seeing her dear old Mum degenerate anymore, she had given in and found the nursing home. All this she had endured, only to be pushed away. No matter how much she told herself her Mum couldn't help it, it still hurt. Slowly, the unfamiliar tears escaped, rolling down her cheek.

Shirley despised women who wallowed. She wiped her eyes and blew her nose briskly. Then she sat quietly until the beauty of her favourite place began to creep its way into her ruffled spirits, and the tightness inside her began to ease a little. As she sat there watching the breeze blowing through the remaining red-gold leaves of autumn, she began cautiously to let her thoughts take shape. She knew that, in her situation, thoughts and feelings were dangerous if given too much sway, but there had to be a time when they came forward to be resolved, to be catalogued and put away in their box neatly, so she could live some kind of a normal life. Relaxing a little, she tried to enjoy the bright morning scene before her. The trees had been so glorious this year, but now many of the leaves were on the ground, slushy and messy in the clear light of the cold morning.

They were no longer gorgeous; but some had remained on the trees and were still clinging now, dappled in rapid sun and shade as the clouds passed swiftly over. Below her in the valley a group of youngsters were huddled together at the base of the war memorial. They seemed to be quarrelling over something; she couldn't see what, and hoped they weren't defacing the monument. It didn't mean an awful lot to her, but she knew it was important to others. In her mind's eye she could see the list of names on it, many of them names that were still familiar in the faces of her neighbours and friends, and at the bottom of the list the usual inscription: "Lest we forget."

"Why?" she thought. "What makes people want to remember the ugliness of war; to go through again the memories of the pain and heartache of loss?"

She jumped as a rocket shrieked its way up into the air, its stars faint and ineffective against the blue-washed sky.

"Fireworks! That's what they're messing about with!"

Bonfire night might be over and done with for everyone else, but they were still trying to recapture the excitement. She smiled to herself, the old rhyme coming to her mind.

"Remember, remember the fifth of November."

She gazed down at the memorial again. It was set in the park near the Parish Church, where last Sunday her daughter had paraded with the Girl Guides, following at a respectful distance the old, dark-suited men, chests thrown out to display proudly the solemn medals, the badges of honour that they wore. Equally proudly on every chest, standing out on the dark background, red as blood, the poppy gave silent witness to the dead. Later, in the church, Shirley had taken communion with the rest, taking comfort in the two-thousand-year-old words: "Do this in remembrance of me."

"Remembrance," she thought. "What makes the difference?

103

Why do some leaves cling and others fall? Why do some memories linger and others fade? There's old Mrs Rogers down the road, now, ten years older than Mum and still helping on committees, doing meals on wheels; and there's my poor old Mum, frail and vacant, sitting in a nursing home, suffering from that ugly thief, Alzheimer's disease."

No, not suffering, not now, anyway. Mercifully, she had little memory of anything that could make her suffer.

Shirley sighed and started the engine. As she turned the car around, she realised with a frisson of guilt that she had no memory of the drive here. Had she gone through any red lights? Had she knocked someone down? She shook herself mentally. Surely she would know if something different had happened. Her secret fears resided in the kind of conversations with her friends that were getting more and more frequent.

"It's awful, you know, I go into a room and completely forget what I'm there for... I've double-booked myself again, forgot to write something down on the calendar... Last week I forgot to pick my son up from school... how can I forget my son? I must be an unnatural mother..."

Shirley didn't think it was unnatural: quite the opposite, really. What was that she'd heard in Church last week?

Can a mother forget the baby at her breast?

Though she may forget, I will not forget you.

See I have engraved you on the palms of my hands.

"Maybe that's the answer," thought Shirley. "Maybe we repeat these things to engrave them on our memories, so that when what's unimportant has gone, we still have the important things to cling to."

With a lingering over-the-shoulder look at her favourite view, she set off to work, her spirits strangely lifted. She decided to go and visit Mum again later. There was no telling; later on, she might not be as bad.

A few miles away, Rachel gazed, puzzled, into the full-length mirror that was in the entrance hall. The image that looked back at her with pale watery eyes didn't fit. She reached forward with the chrysanthemums that were clutched, dripping, in her right hand, and scrubbed at the image: but it didn't help, it still didn't fit. Rachel knew – knew without trying to know – that the reflection was of a young woman in a white dress made of parachute silk, holding a bunch of fragrant Sweet Peas. Though she couldn't make any sense of what her eyes were telling her, she recognised that the parchment-faced old woman dressed in nothing but a thin petticoat was not real.

Suddenly, behind her, a burgundy uniform with a person-shape inside it began to speak. "Oh, there you are, Rachel, I've been looking all over for you. Come on, love; I'll take you back up. Give me the Chrysanths – they're a bit mashed, what have you been doing? Dear dear, you've broken the vase. You haven't hurt yourself, have you? Don't worry, I'll clean up the mess in a minute."

Rachel allowed the burgundy uniform to take her arm. As she turned away from the mirror, the fragrance of the Sweet Peas brought tears of joy to her eyes.

"It's my wedding day today," she said, as she allowed herself to be led away.

The Odd-Sock Fairy

It all started when my girl Lucy couldn't find her old primary school socks. Well, to be more precise, when she couldn't find *one* of her old primary school socks. I suppose you might think it odd, considering Lucy left primary school all of twelve years ago; and not that there was anything special about the socks themselves either, they were just ordinary white ankle socks. Apart from the fact that they ponged a bit, there was only one thing that made them special: Gareth had signed them.

Well, he'd signed *one* of them.

"Honestly, Mum, you're hopeless! Where have you put it?"

"I don't know. Why do you need it?"

She cast me a withering look.

"Because it's blue, of course!"

Blue? That was odd, I could have sworn they were white… but it was the assumption that *I'd* put it somewhere that grabbed me. It's always the same. If something isn't washed in time, it's my fault. If the Shreddy-Pops run out halfway through breakfast, it's my fault, and if something's lost… you get the picture? Yes, you and a million other mums, so if you are one of that million I don't need to say any more, do I? You know exactly where Lucy's special sock was. So did I, naturally; but for the benefit of everyone else: "The Odd-Sock Fairy's eaten it," I said.

Lucy threw me that old-fashioned, I'm-grown-up-now look that they all perfect after their body-clock strikes Thirteen.

"Don't mess me around, Mum. This is important!"

Of course it's important.

"Define important," I said, hopefully.

She rounded on me fiercely.

106

"I mean important, Really, *really* important. I need it for tomorrow, and I need it for Saturday, and if you don't understand that, then you're not a Proper Mother."

I was impressed. She hardly ever plays the Not-a-Proper-Mother card.

"Well, darling," I said, calmly (it annoys her *dreadfully* when I stay calm), "I shall do my level best to find it."

By this time, she had reached the point where she was pulling stuffed shoe boxes out of the bottom of the cupboard and spilling the contents all over the living room floor. I could hear her muttered imprecations quite clearly.

"It's always the same in this house. It's a madhouse. You can never find anything when you want it." She yelped and jumped back as a big spider fled in all its ferocity across the growing piles of her life history.

"Now look at that! That's exactly what I mean. This place is a health hazard. It's a wonder I ever made it past the nappy stage!"

Yes, I thought that was a wonder, too: but I remembered that old saying about wisdom being the better part of discretion – or no, is it the other way round? Anyway, I didn't agree with her. Not out loud.

"You know what I'm going to do?" she said then, rounding on me and threatening me with an ancient Christmas cracker – still loaded, apparently – "I'm going to call the telly and get the Muck-Busters in! *They'll* soon clean up this pigsty, and then all the neighbours will know what you're like, and you'll probably *die* of shame."

She seemed to derive a vast amount of comfort from this idea.

"You needn't think I don't mean it," she said, wagging the increasingly droopy cracker like a fat red finger. "You've had this coming to you for a long time. It's about time you had some professionals in to Sort You Out!"

"Careful," I said, "it might go off in a minute. You'll be done for assault with a deadly festive accessory…" I started to chuckle. "…and *it* will be done for being an accessory to the crime."

Her lips twitched; but with an admirable effort, she maintained her anger.

"Oh, it's hopeless talking to you. I'm going to Gareth's, and I'm going to phone Muck-Busters as soon as I get there."

"But Lucy," I called after her as she stormed out, "even if you call them now, I don't think they'll be here by Saturday."

She *has* been a little up and down lately. I suppose it's only to be expected, under the circumstances, but being the so-laid-back-I'm-positively-recumbent type, I find it difficult to understand.

She's probably right: I'm not a Proper Mother.

Anyway, after she stormed out of the house, I surveyed the wreckage that was once my living room floor. A Proper Mother would, at that point, have started tidying up Lucy's life history – shedding a few sentimental tears in the process – and would have combed the house to find the offending sock: but not I. I just strolled into the kitchen and spoke into the vague area between the dishwasher and the washing machine.

"She means it, you know, about the Muck-Busters. Just imagine if they *did* come. What would your life be like?"

I paused and turned my back politely for a moment, then turned round again and casually pulled open the door of the washing machine.

I reached in and took the sock.

"Now, you're not up to your old tricks, are you?" I said, still talking toward the washing machine. "If I go upstairs to match this with the other one, you won't have been there before me, will you?"

There was no reply: but the silence took on an injured expression.

"Don't come the old innocent with me, Miss!" I said. "This is too important to worry about your hurt feelings. I don't want to go upstairs to Lucy's old room and find that you've taken the matching sock in place of this one."

The silence grew stony.

"That's all very well," I said, "but *I* remember the lacy gloves, even if you don't. I know very well that as soon as you returned the first one to my sewing box, you had its pair out of my sock drawer before I could say knife."

The air was definitely sulky by this time.

"I suppose I should just be thankful that you haven't tucked into it yet. What a nightmare that would have been." I turned to go.

That's when the voice stopped me.

"That's a complete fallacy," it said, dripping with the disdain that all true fairies have for humans.

I turned in surprise.

There she was, sitting on the curve of the front loader as if it were a hammock, dangling one chunky leg over the edge. She was by no means your conventional fairy, and for a moment the sight of her took my breath away.

"What's the matter?" she snapped. "Lost your power of speech? About time too; someone else might be able to get a word in now and then."

We looked at each other for a telling moment.

"Well," she said pettishly, as if I had spoken, "there wasn't much point in hiding any more, was there? You've obviously known about me all along. I used to hear you when I lived under the children's beds, 'Ask Santa for more socks, girls, the Odd-Sock Fairy's taken all yours.' Huh. What a way to educate your kiddies. Pack o' lies." She sniffed.

I found my tongue. "Was it indeed?"

She shrugged. "Not really. I did take most of 'em, especially in the winter. Well, a body's got to keep herself warm somehow – even more so, now I've moved location."

I acknowledged that it must get a bit damp inside the workings of the washing machine, but she didn't look to me as if she ought to suffer much from the cold. She was definitely – how can I put this in modern parlance? Girthily Challenged? Weightily Formed? I would say a Cosy Armful, which is much more *warm,* somehow: but there was nothing cosy about her at all. Her hair, a lurid shade of lime green, was spiked up – using my fabric softener, by the smell of it – and she was dressed in an ankle-length, shapeless knitted dress, the colour of washing-machine sludge, that stretched over her ample figure and clung in all the wrong places.

I must have shown my disfavour in my face, for she suddenly grimaced at me. "I could always snatch it back, you know, and then you'd be in the soup!"

"So would you," I countered. "Remember Muck-Busters."

She pulled a long face and resting her elbow on her bent knee and her chin in her hand, she looked up at me slantways. "Ok, I won't take it back. Not because of Muck-Busters, but because I'm curious. Why does Lucy need her old sock so desperately?"

I sighed. "You'll never believe this, but she needs it for her something blue."

"Blue?" she said, puzzled. "But it's white!"

I shook my head sadly. "Not anymore, it's not. Look."

I lifted the revolting thing up for her to see and watched the understanding dawn on her face. Like me, the Sock Fairy was still seeing the socks as they were when Lucy first brought them home from the last day of Primary school, pristine white except where her pals (including Gareth) had signed them. But since then, Lucy had worn them on various special occasions until they got too small and wearing them on sweaty feet inside cheap black dance shoes had made the shoe dye rub off, turning the feet distinctly blue.

"She and Gareth are getting married on Saturday. Tomorrow's her hen night and she wants to show them off to the girls; and on Saturday—"

"Ahh," said my well-formed fairy friend. "Something old, something new, something borrowed – and something blue!"

The fairy wrinkled her nose. "A bit of blue cheese would do just as well. I haven't washed it, you know."

"Heaven forbid! The signatures would come off."

The Odd-Sock Fairy laughed heartily, flapping her incongruously flimsy wings as if to leave.

"Wait," I said. "What was the fallacy?"

"Pardon?"

"When you first deigned to appear, you said, 'that's a complete fallacy'…"

"Oh. You always told the girls that I *ate* their socks. I don't eat 'em…"

Suddenly, I recognised the sludge-coloured dress.

"…I *wear* 'em."

"I see," I said thoughtfully, looking at her well-rounded figure. "So – what *do* you eat?"

"Well, you know all those bits and pieces that leap from the frying pan and throw themselves down that little gap behind the cooker?"

"You?" I asked.

"Me."

I nodded. No wonder she didn't want Muck-Busters to call.

111

The wedding went off without a hitch, unless you count the faint aroma of blue cheese as the bride glided up the aisle on her Dad's arm.

Even dear Gareth was immaculate, his face lighting up touchingly as he stood, tall and boyishly handsome, watching her walk up the aisle. But I felt myself stiffen as my gaze focused on his footwear.

That damned fairy!

He appeared to be wearing odd socks.

The Waiting Room

It was the lie that always bothered me most. The rest of it I coped with; the fuss, the choices, the furtive discussion about what to expect on the night. Poor Mum: she got so embarrassed talking to me about it. Well, we didn't so much in those days, did we? It's all so different now.

I coped with choosing the dress. I coped with handling prima donna bridesmaids, what they would consider wearing and what they wouldn't. I coped with Dad worrying about the speeches, and Aunts and Uncles whose feelings were slighted over some triviality or other.

It was the lie that fazed me.

It was absolutely fine at the rehearsal, do you remember? That's because it wasn't the real thing, you see. There we were, giggling with embarrassment, interrupting each other; the men making suggestive jokes, the girls blushing and flirting openly. I skimmed by it: they were only words, they didn't mean anything – until that day.

On that day, as I stood at the altar and made that vow to Love, I knew it was a lie: and I started to cry.

I'm not much of a religious person; I've never thought about God, really, before or since: but that lie… it came out of my mouth and hung in the air, like an indictment against me. It was as if some celestial Being was flinging it back in my face: a heavenly challenge from someone that knew all about Love and its meaning. It allowed honour; it smiled gently on obey; but Love…

Someone knew I was lying.

It didn't matter, really. It's not unusual for a woman to cry at her own wedding: in fact, I think I probably set everyone else off. The moment passed, I wiped my eyes, you slipped the ring on my finger, your emotion brimming

113

in spite of your desire to hide it from mocking eyes, and we carried on.

I carried on.

Jem.

You've always been a good wife to me. You've looked after me the way you know I needed looking after. You've shown love to me, Sarah, even when you wanted to turn away. Do you think I didn't know that you married me because you wanted a way out?

I suppose girls these days would laugh at me, so scared of life as I was. Today's girl would leave home, get a flat with her friends, find a job in London, or something: but I couldn't do that. I was far too shy; I lacked self-confidence. Girls didn't do that much even then, despite women's lib. and all that. It was a long time before anything so – so *dashing* was expected of any but the really brave ones – and I wasn't brave, was I? Living in the shadow of my brother and sisters, I felt like the archetypal ugly duckling. So, when you asked me, it seemed like a wonderful escape from an overbearing family. That was the one thing that girls like me *did* do, so it was ironic that it plunged me into the biggest fight of my life, wasn't it? Mum couldn't believe I would turn down Michael Carter from the Carter chain of Antique shops in favour of Jeremy Alsop, a factory worker. I knew that if it came to a choice between him and you, I would choose you. I knew you were a gentleman, you see. It's a good word, isn't it? Gentle man. That's what you are. Mum didn't see it that way, though. She was livid. I was letting the side down, wasn't I? It seems so daft now, but I nearly didn't get away with it. It was Dad who swung it, really. He rarely spoke out against Mum, but he was so good. I'll never forget that. I think he knew that Michael was a cruel man… and what an escape! His poor wife… what a dreadful time she's had with him.

Such a dreadful time. Is this a dreadful time?

I can't say that about me, even though I've spent most of my married life living with that lie. I can't say I've really been unhappy. I married you knowing that you would always be kind, and I haven't been disappointed in that. My only trouble has been ensuring that you haven't let me have my own way too much. You kept saying you were happy if I was happy; but I know that I must have been difficult to please sometimes. Lots of times. We've had our spats, haven't we, but you always supported me when I was down, and shared in all my little excitements, and we had the joy of bringing up two children together. But it's so sad that it was all based on a lie.

I can't believe that. Love isn't like that, Sarah. Love is about choice, not feelings. You chose to commit to me all those years ago, and you've kept those vows. I know I don't deserve your love, and I'm sorry that I couldn't make you feel the passion every girl dreams of, but you've loved me with a greater love than that, because it was selfless.

Such a surprise then, to find myself here, now, in this waiting room. That's what it is, you know, it's a waiting room. It feels temporary, with its non-committal magnolia walls and unthreatening, sterile floor. Sitting here, it feels as if time has stopped. I've felt like that ever since they told me. Time has stopped. There's a moment when it's moving, and then they say, *"**there's been an accident**,"* and it stops; you feel it stop at ***accident***. There's no time here, there's only the accident. I suppose you feel like that too – do you feel like that, Jem? Can you feel?

I can feel.

Can you feel my hand holding yours?

I wonder if you can hear me.

I can hear.

I don't know whether you can or not: but there's

something I have to put straight. It's not the time for lies now. The truth is the truth whether anyone hears it or not, and it's important that I say this:

Please don't, Sarah... don't say something you might regret. I'm in a dark place, love, and I need you. Don't leave me now. I can feel inside this place, and I can hear: I can even sense your pain, but there's nothing I can do to take it away. I don't understand what's happened to me, but I'm helpless. You're the only reality for me now. Without you there'd be no point in hanging on.

I just want to say, I was wrong. All those years I've wasted, believing what I've believed, and the moment they told me I knew. I knew like a knife going into my heart. I used to think that love was about your heart beating fast and getting all flushed and excited. I used to think it was like a stabbing, yearning pain inside, an ache that was sweet and bitter all at once, and I used to regret that I hadn't felt that way about you.

I was wrong.

The lie was in the wrong place.

The moment they told me you'd been in the accident, I knew; knew with a terrible, yearning, gaping fear how much, how so very much I love you. Love must have crept up on me without my noticing because it's here, here inside me now, tearing at my very being. Maybe that Someone at our wedding is having the last laugh. Maybe He's saying, I hold you to your vow, Sarah, you vowed to love, and love him you will, in spite of what you thought then.

I've looked at your face a million times without really seeing it, and here I am in this waiting room, drinking in every breath you take, every laboured, rhythmic gasp of the pump that's feeding your lungs. I'm watching over you for the slightest twitch of muscle, the merest flick of eye. I count your lashes, and it doesn't seem an odd thing to do. I wish I could turn the clock back. I wish it was yesterday, and I knew, so that I could tell you: but it isn't yesterday, and I'm not the Lord of time; so you have to get better, do you hear me? You must get better so that I can let you know how much I love you. You mustn't give up.

I'll never give up.

There's so much I want to say that I've not said, but I'm not going to say it until I know you're listening.

I'm listening.

They told me to talk to you, you know. Talk to him, they said. It doesn't matter what. Read a recipe book to him, it won't make any difference, it's just the sound of your voice. What you say doesn't matter.

Sometimes I think they're wrong, I think it does matter: and sometimes, well, it all seems so pointless, and I want them to turn off the machines now, so I have all the pain at once. That's odd, isn't it? I didn't know that hope could be so frightening, that it carries those unbearable times when you're afraid that it's all going to be in vain. If they turned off the machines then I wouldn't have to endure the hope anymore – but then, I can't bear that you die without knowing that I love you.

I'm not going to die. There's so much to live for.

Jem? Jem, is that you?

Jem, if that was you, do it again!

There's so much to live for.

Nurse – Nurse, come quickly! I felt his fingers – I really did – he squeezed my hand...

First published by *Writing Magazine*; winner of the Love Story competition.

The Storyteller

Nobody knew where she came from, or if she had a home at all. She always said her home was the story, woven carefully over time like a tapestry. A stitch here, a knot there; a fine thread or a thick one, all added judiciously to form a person, a village, a landscape. She always came alone, although the pedlar who forded the river every month seemed to know when she was coming. Once or twice a year he would wipe the ale from his beard and say laconically, "Marta's on her way."

The whisper would run around the village quickly.

"Marta's coming."

"Did you hear? Marta's on her way."

The village Elder would order kindling to be collected for the bonfire. One of the farmers would kill a pig in readiness, scoring the fat so it would crackle sweetly over the fire, its juices running into the ashes; and Leon's mouth would water in response. The women would bake, the men gather. Sometimes the feast would be extravagant, sometimes less so; but always it would bring the community together.

Leon couldn't remember a time that he didn't long for Marta. She seemed to have been a presence in his life from before he was born, the vibrations of her voice a muffled strumming in his Mama's womb, the formless words curling around him like a hazy memory, cocooning him with warmth and emotion, zest and excitement. Her coming was the highlight of his life; he couldn't remember a time when it wasn't. As a boy, he had wriggled as close to her knee as possible, watching in fascination as her hands wove hazel switches into a basket above his head, and her voice, treacle-warm, wove a tale that stirred his heart.

When she arrived, the bonfire would be lit, and her host

would bow or curtsey and say, "Storyteller, will you honour my humble home with your presence until the sun sets too soon and the Well of Stories has run dry?"

And Marta would bow her head briefly, her long dark plaits giving her an air of serenity, and she would answer, "Whilst the sun exists, the Well cannot run dry; but I accept your hospitality until it's time to leave. May your home be blessed."

The host always received one of Marta's most beautiful baskets as thanks for their hospitality. She wove them as she spoke, and to Leon it seemed that her stories were part of the very fabric of them. His mother had many baskets, but only two were from Marta's hands, and only two were used and displayed. The others, not by Marta's hands, were hidden from disapproving eyes, until Leon could smuggle them out and sell them at the market.

When Leon was nine, he had announced to his family that he wanted to be a storyteller.

His father had looked up from his meal and grunted.

"You are a farmer. You cannot be a storyteller."

"But father—"

"You are a farmer. This farm will pass to you. That is your destiny, as it is mine to build and tend so that there is enough to give to your brothers and your sister. This farm is your future, as it is their support. This farm is your duty. Storytelling, pah! Storytelling is women's work."

Leon had stolen away to the children's den and had told them a story of a talking dog and a fiery dragon. The mothers had searched for their children to put them to bed, in vain. Spellbound, the children had gone home tardily, most of them awakening in the night from starlit dreams of anthropomorphic animals.

Leon's father, furious from the complaints of his neighbours, had taken a hazel switch and thrashed his eldest

119

son. "You cannot be a storyteller, Leon. That is the end of it."

That year when he was nine was the last time Yara had been Marta's hostess. Leon had spent every spare hour seeking her out.

"How do you do what you do?" he asked.

"The basket or the stories?"

"Both."

Marta sighed a long sigh. "The basket weaving I can show you, it is a skill that can be learned. The stories..." she picked up her half-completed basket. "You see, Leon? This is real, it is tangible, I can show you how the frame is made, how each switch weaves over and under. Anyone can make a basket, and it will be a good, useful basket if you practice enough. But stories – they are woven from the fabric of life, mixed with the realms of dreams and imagination; they are truth dressed up in shimmering fantasy; they are whimsical and evocative like a will o' the wisp. You cannot pin down a story, it meanders where it will. I can't teach you how to weave a story; either you are a storyteller – or you are not."

Leon looked at the ground, silent.

Marta sighed again. "Perhaps I can teach a few dramatic techniques, but you can only be a storyteller if it is who you are."

She looked at him thoughtfully.

"Here," she said, handing him the basket frame. "Come to me every evening before bedtime, and I will show you how to make baskets."

So, after supper every night, Leon went to where she slept in the hayloft over the barn, and she taught him to weave baskets. While they wove, she told him stories of life; of babies stolen by river creatures, of evil men who hunted and stole and received their just deserts; stories of

120

fantasy, of impish fairies who stole the butter and curdled the milk, stories of evil wizards and brave knights.

And Leon learned how to weave.

If his father were to thrash him now, it could only be by Leon's consent, for the boy had grown into a man, hard and strong; but the habit of obedience had worn a groove in Leon's desire. He farmed and he ate, he took the animals to market and courted the market trader's daughter. But despite all this, there was a small part of him that wove stories stubbornly, in his head alone.

This night, Marta, her dark plaits streaked with fine strands of white, stood by the fire. Yara stepped forward. "Storyteller, will you honour my humble home with your presence until the sun sets too soon and the Well of Stories has run dry?"

Marta bowed her head. "Whilst the sun exists, the Well cannot run dry; but I accept your hospitality until it's time to leave. May your home be blessed."

The villagers went to prepare the feast while Marta followed Yara home.

"Where is my friend Leon?" asked Marta.

"He is not yet back from the market," said Yara.

"He went to market? Didn't he know I was coming?"

"Simanen said... he thought..." Yara looked at her husband helplessly.

Simanen spoke. "The boy has forgotten about stories. It is better if we do not stir that nest. Storytelling is women's work; I don't want him getting distracted."

Marta nodded.

"I understand," she said.

"I don't think you do," said Yara. "I know what you think, and you are wrong. Whatever his desires may have been as a boy, there is no doubt; Leon went to market willingly. He was even hoping to stay overnight with the market trader's daughter." She looked at her husband. "We think – we are hoping—"

Simanen interrupted. "He is to be betrothed to her. It is a good match."

Marta smiled. "Of course."

That night, as the villagers, sated on a feast of roasted pork and apple cider, sat or reclined around the bonfire, Marta picked up a basket frame and began her story.

"There once was a girl whose name was Tarma. Tarma wasn't particularly clever, nor was she comfortable with women's work. Her baking was legendary – in the sense it was to be avoided. Her beauty was celebrated – by her mother alone. There was but one thing that Tarma could do with skill. Tarma could weave stories. A wonderful thing, yes? But in those days, things were different. Storytelling was different. So Tarma's mother scolded her for her inattention, and her father beat her for disobedience. Her family scorned her as a dreamer. 'You cannot be a storyteller,' they said. 'How can this be? It is shameful for you to even want such a thing. Storytelling is a very important thing, a thing that only a man can be trusted to do. What might happen to you if you wander around from village to village alone? You might be eaten by a bear, or attacked by wicked men. You would be at risk from evil spirits. A dragon might find you, and there would be none to protect you. You cannot be a storyteller, it isn't decent."

The villagers murmured together. Some of them laughed. Whoever heard of a man being a storyteller? How clever of Marta to flip the truth on its head like that!

"Tarma was devasted. When Enfredo, the storyteller, came to her village, she pleaded with him to help her. 'I cannot,' he said. 'How can I help you? The very food in my mouth comes from your friends and family. How can I betray their trust like that?

122

'I cannot encourage you, except to say this. If you are a storyteller, the stories will come whether you will or no. You can despise them, suppress them, bury them as deep as the colourless creatures of the sea, but they will find a way out. I cannot teach you storytelling. All I can teach you is how to weave baskets.' "

Marta lifted her head and laid down her basket for a moment. She stared into the trees, where the dark form of a young man could be seen in the shadows.

"Time went on, and Tarma forgot her dream of being a storyteller. Her daily life drew her in. She married, and soon there was a child on the way. The stories that came to her when she was young receded, appearing only in fevered dreams. She was content with her lot; certainly, her life was uneventful, but it was also untouched by tragedy. No bear, no dragon, no evil spirit or wilful wickedness touched her life; but then, two things occurred. Firstly, the man to whom she had given everything was exposed as a fraud. He had stolen, cheated and lied; and the worst lie of all was that he had another wife – a wife and family two villages away. The village cast him out, and the girl was left alone with her baby. Her despair knew no bounds. She was untethered. She was neither wife nor maiden; she had not chosen to be what she now was, but she was spurned as if she had. She spent much of her time alone, going to the river for water in the heat of the afternoon, when everyone else was asleep.

"One afternoon, the sun was hot as she carried her baby with her to the river. The child, nearly two years old now, seemed heavier than usual, and Tarma was very tired. She drew her water, then she sat on the bank of the river and watched it flow by, as she had many times before. It gave her peace. It seemed to her that the river was like her life, sometimes, as now, flowing smooth and peaceful; at other times, murky and dark, and yet others turbulent, dangerous and traumatic. Half asleep, she pondered, wondering what she could do, listening to the gentle lap of the rivulets on the bank, watching the river as if it were time slipping by, and then, all at once, her thoughts were ripped open by the sound of screams. Her daughter, curious and wakeful, had toddled to the river's edge. She looked up to see her child, her precious, beloved girl, all bloodied and ominously quiet now within the jaws of a river creature."

The villagers were silent. From one woman came a sob of sympathy. From the trees, the young man began to move forward as if drawn by a cord.

"What did she do?" someone asked, in hushed tones.

"She did everything she could. She took a rock, waded into the river and threw it at the river creature, fruitlessly – for it had disappeared, leaving a rapidly dispersing pool of her daughter's blood. She found a stick and dragged it along the riverbed; hysterical, she dove and dove again, hoping to see – hoping to find…"

Marta took a shuddering breath.

"But it was too late. Both child and creature were gone, taken by the treacherous water."

Marta paused. The villagers sat silent, waiting.

"For a while, Tarma wandered in the forest, following the river, always following the river, looking for her lost child. She never returned to her village. But one day, she came upon Enfredo. He took pity upon her, taking her in. He listened to her piercing sorrow until her ravings quieted, and she began once again to live; a strange sort of half-life: half real, half dream.

"Enfredo was wonderful to her. He showed her how to take her experience and weave it into something useful, much as I weave this basket. He taught her that every story is made up of life's tragedies and triumphs. How even the oldest stories are given a stitch here, a knot there, like an ever-changing tapestry in the hands of a master. But most of all, he taught her that a storyteller is born, not made.

"Tarma travelled with Enfredo, learning his ways. When he died, Tarma buried him with honour, and took over his work. At first the villagers were shocked. Even though they had seen her with Enfredo, and heard her stories, it seemed outrageous that she, a woman, could be a storyteller. But eventually, the stories wove their magic, and the villagers accepted her. How could they not? For a storyteller must be a storyteller, and cannot be denied, even if the story is only told to the wind in the trees."

"Is this your story? Your true story?" Leon had crept forward from the shadow of the trees and was standing before Marta in the centre of the circle.

"All good stories contain truth. But this one is as unvarnished as I could make it."

"I'm coming with you."

Marta smiled.

Simanen stepped forward.

"Hear me, boy! If you do this, you are no longer my son!"

"Father I—"

"No longer my son, you understand? The farm will go to your next brother. The market girl will be his, not yours. Make your choice."

There was a long silence.

"Then so be it."

Leon went and stood by Marta. His father stepped forward and spat on the ground before turning his back.

"Thus your story begins," said Marta. "You have only to learn how best to weave it."

62 Steps

The girl sat on the buff stone terrace in the white heat of the Mediterranean summer. Every so often, she glanced toward the horizon, her eyes brushing past the decaying walls that did not have the romance of history to give them stature. She ignored, too, the quiet winding road that nestled, almost out of sight, under the café's own terrace walls; and the drying foliage that grew haphazardly further down the hill. It was the horizon that drew her gaze. Deftly, her hands moved as she sketched outlines, and as the sun moved steadily round behind her as if to take a stealthy peek over her shoulder, she added colour and form, eyes moving back and forth without breaking concentration. Thirst edged its way into her consciousness, but the light was just right, and she did not dare break the moment.

Julia could not resist a glance at the painting as she picked up the phone, the familiar trepidation hovering. She hated making phone calls, but if it was to be done, she would have to do it herself. She hadn't even bothered to discuss it with Mark; she knew what the answer would be.

"Ring them up and ask them, if it bothers you that much. I don't care – as long as we have a double bed…"

In her imagination she saw his lascivious grin. No matter that they were taking the children with them; Mark like to get romantic on holiday. His only question about the accommodation was to do with the sleeping arrangements. To have had to share a room with his two little treasures would have spoiled the point.

Determinedly, Julia dialled the agent's number; but she needn't have bothered. The travel agent was polite but firm.

"I'm sorry, Mrs Howard, that's the only accommodation available, there's really nothing else. In fact you were lucky to get that at this late stage."

126

She wove a whole coffee-break conversation out of that one phone call, imagining the agents raising knowing eyebrows over these idiots who wanted the Ritz for peanuts. She pulled the brochure towards her and read the offending paragraph once more.

> Beautiful first-floor family accommodation, sleeps four. Delightful location 15 minutes walk uphill from the town. Sea view. Well worth the climb.*
>
> *As this accommodation is reached by a total of 62 steps, it is not suitable for the elderly or infirm.

Julia was tired; she needed a holiday. Mark needed one even more. Sarah and Biddy were at that age where they could slow the whole family down to a wearing crawl; where it was easier for Biddy, big as she was, to be carried than to hang around waiting for her to catch up. She looked again at the painting which hung on the wall, noting that it was slightly dusty. The colours had faded a little over the years: she hadn't noticed before, the occasional fond glance being enough to bring alive the wonder of those golden days.

Now, when she most needed the jewel-studded memories, all Julia could recall was the Island heat; the thirst that could suddenly descend; the fact that there was no drinking water in its taps.

Sixty-two Steps.

Sixty-two steps at the top of a hill. A hill could be gentle and rolling, or it could be steep.

Sixty-two steps with tired children, crabby parents, and several heavy bottles of water every day.

She scolded herself, knowing that she was seeing the worst possible scenario, but she couldn't help sending up a pleading prayer. Please, please let it be all right. Let it be upgraded at the last minute, or something. It's too important.

The girl leaned back and studied her handiwork, reaching absently for the bottle of water that was on the table beside her. Eyes still flickering back and forth from the image to the original, she swigged from the bottle, grimacing slightly. In the time it had stood there, it had grown somewhat tepid; but it was still welcome for all that. She stretched and allowed herself the pleasure of enjoying the view for its own sake. She drank it in, warm, indescribably lovely, savouring the peace, the beauty; committing to her memory not only the sight, but the sound and smells that made the whole so magical. The cicadas were making their noisy chirrup; waiters called to one another, laughing, their white teeth flashing in their handsome, tanned faces.

Only two days left.

For fourteen years, Julia had dreamed of returning to the Island, but there was always a stumbling-block. First it was the mortgage, eating every penny of both salaries; then it was all the expenses that children bring. Shoes, coats, trips, tuition fees. It all ate into the budget. Two years previously, Mark had got a bonus, and they'd booked a last-minute deal to a different island – they couldn't find a holiday to her Island anywhere: but one island, surely, must be much like another.

It wasn't.

Biddy was ill for a week and turned overnight from a plump little toddler to a skinny child. The second week she

128

developed an inexplicable prejudice against the food, and wore a cavernous hungry look until they found somewhere that had baked beans and tomato ketchup. The scenery was depressing, the area touristy; the weather broke as soon as Biddy was well and it was the coldest September the locals could remember.

Mark smiled and made it fun, skimming stones into the rolling waves, his hood up against the stinging rain.

"I don't care, love," he said, "as long as I'm with you, it's still a holiday. Come on, let's go down to the bar."

The highlight of the holiday was the one nightcap they dared indulge in at the poolside bar, where the owner stood huddled in his winter woollies, and the turnover of holiday faces was quicker than a supermarket checkout queue. It was a measure of their love for each other that it was still a good holiday. They laughed at the ripples the wind made across the deserted pool. They laughed at the childishly coquettish way Biddy responded to the Greek doctor's charm. They laughed at the baked beans and the Tea-like-Mama-Makes signs. It rained: they shrugged.

"So what? It's Greek rain. It's different."

No-one spoke of disappointment, but when Julia got back home, she had looked at the painting and sighed wistfully. All this was in the back of her mind as, defeated, she closed the brochure.

It was strange, really. The doubt had only set in when Mark phoned, jubilant, to tell her the news.

"You'll never guess what I've found! I've gone ahead and booked it – it's only a week, but we're going at last. I've booked us a holiday to your Island!"

Even as she shrieked with joy, the thought jumped into her mind that it wouldn't be the same, and as if he'd heard her thoughts, Mark sobered down.

"I don't want to sound negative, but it might have

changed, you know. It *is* fourteen years since you were there."

She shouldered her bag, the watercolour tucked safely in the bottom, and walked down into her favourite cove. There, seated on a flat rock, she gazed at the timeless, unchanging scene around her. It was the sense of history that amazed her. You could look at the islets and know how they must have looked when first they were formed. You could imagine them rising up, majestic and eternal, out of the roiling ocean, and you could wonder at how they, mere naked rocks in the beginning, had clothed themselves with colour and light over the long passing of the quiet years.

She had never known peace quite like it.

In the eternal six weeks before departure, Julia struggled with her wildly swinging emotions. Surely it was wrong to want something so much? One day it seemed that only disillusion waited there; another day tremors of excitement caught her and set her laughing at nothing. She didn't know from hour to hour which feeling would be lying hidden, ready to pounce if she let down her guard.

Having built the Island as a dream, she now tried to prepare her family for disappointed expectations.

"It's very small, girls, there won't be a kid's club, you know."

"S'alright," said Sarah, "kid's clubs are *boring*. I'd rather go swimming."

"There isn't a swimming pool."

"There's a beach, isn't there?" said Mark.

Julia nodded.

"There are lots. Quiet little coves around every corner, but most of them are shingle. Only one or two are sandy."

Mark shrugged.

130

"There's water, that's the important thing."

"There isn't, though."

"What?"

"Water. To drink, I mean. The Island doesn't have fresh water, there's only salt water in the taps."

"We'll have to buy bottled, then. At least there's plenty of water for the kids to swim."

He looked at Julia's face.

"It *is* safe for them to swim, I suppose?"

Julia nodded, gulping.

"Oh yes, but we'll have to watch out for the sea-urchins."

"Sea-urchins?"

"Spiky sea creatures. You have to be careful not to step on them, or it'll ruin your holiday. We'll have to get swim shoes. Not just the children, all of us."

Mark looked at her, the twinkle lurking at the back of his eyes.

"Hmm. Limited menus, shingle beaches, lethal sea creatures, no sense of time, nothing to do, no water, no swimming pool. Tell me, my love, why are we going?"

"I don't know," said Julia.

"I do," said Mark, taking her by the shoulders and propelling her to where the painting was hanging. "That's why we're going – that up there. Because it's your Island,. It's special to you, and what's special to you is special to us, too."

"But you might not like it!"

Mark sighed, exasperated.

"You've been going on about this place since before we were married. If I don't like it…" He grinned, shrugging. "…at least we'll know!"

As the boat drew out of the port, she photographed the memory on her mind. The sea was dark, sapphire blue, the island rising like a green and amber jewel from its depths. Tears pricked her eyes, but they were sentimental, not bitter. She was ready to go home, but it was with a sense of regret. As the morning light on the Island grew stronger, the boat drew further and further away. For her, there would never be another place quite like this one; and one day, she would return. She took the painting out of her bag and promised herself that wherever she went, it would have pride of place so that the memory would never fade.

Two days to go. She couldn't find the passports, the children's shorts came out crumpled and dirty from the bottom of their wardrobes, the head teacher was kicking up about days off school, and Julia was thoroughly cross, muttering under her breath.

"I wish we weren't going. It's a mistake to try and go back. There so much to do, and it's only for a week. It's hardly worth all the hassle."

However, the next day it seemed as if her idle wish had been granted. Mark lay in bed, his face grey. All he wanted to do was sleep.

"You go on your own, darling," he said. "Take the children and go. I'll be all right."

For a moment, the temptation was there in front of her; but Julia knew she couldn't do it. It wouldn't feel right to go without him. Anyway, surely he was just being noble? He'd probably feel betrayed if she took him at his word. She shook her head.

"I can't do that. It wouldn't be the same without you. I want you to share it."

Even as she said it, she knew it was true. He was part of her now, and without him it couldn't possibly be special. She bundled him into the passenger seat of the car and drove him to the surgery, swallowing the lump in her throat. She wouldn't make him feel bad by crying. Her treacherous feelings had changed again: how *could* she have said she didn't want to go?

Mark sat there huddled in the chair while Dr Davis examined him.

"It's a virus. Two or three days, plenty of fluids..."

Her heart sinking, she explained about the holiday and asked for a note to claim on the insurance. The doctor raised his eyebrows.

"Do you *want* to cancel it?"

She choked back the tears.

"No, but there's not much point if he's ill, is there?"

"Pah, don't worry about that, I can give him something that'll help him feel better. Just make sure he gets plenty of rest that's all. You can drive to the airport, can't you?"

Julia nodded. Her heart was light once again.

Uncomplaining, thankful that they were going after all, she coped with all the packing, sorting the cat, the newspapers, the milk; then the three hour night drive to the airport, finding the car park, checking in, knowing that for good or for ill, the Island would be there at the end of it. All through the nightmare journey, she doggedly did it all: hauling suitcases in the dark, chivvying children drunk with sleep, hanging around on quaysides. Hour after interminable hour they travelled on, the bright-faced reps jollying them along. Apology followed apology, given with bright smiles as buses turned up full, ferries were late and connections were missed. Finally, beyond weariness, they reached the Island just as the sun was beginning to set. Grey-faced and bleary-eyed from lack of sleep, Mark turned to her as they pulled slowly into the pretty port, the sea below them darkening to a midnight blue like the stone in her engagement ring.

"Well," he said, his tired smile tentative, "has it changed?"

She shook her head.

"No," she said; but the spark wasn't there, and she couldn't hide it. He took her hand.

"Give it time," he said. "You're tired. It's been a long journey."

Julia didn't respond. There were still the sixty-two steps.

The bus dropped them a long way up the hill. It was very steep, the road was narrow, and the steps stretched up before them. Slowly, with frequent rests, they toiled their way up. On and on they laboured, the gate banging shut behind them like the jaws of some wild beast. One foot, then another foot, plod, plod, plod they climbed, Biddy whinging tiredly, Sarah, still annoyingly full of beans, climbing precariously on the walls. Julia's calves were aching, her knees creaking and trembling in protest.

Out of breath, hot, sticky and unbearably tired, they finally reached a wide courtyard. There was no-one to greet them. No-one around at all. Timidly they approached the silent building, peering at the numbers on the doors.

"We must be up there," said Mark, pointing to the first floor flat.

Julia groaned.

"My poor knees – I should have joined the gym!"

Mark gave her a quizzical look.

"Wouldn't a step class have been of more use?"

They began to climb again, two short flights that were aeons long, until they reached a balcony that turned back on itself and ran around the front of the building. As Julia stepped onto the white concrete, clasping the railing for support, she could hold back the words no longer. As she rounded the corner they burst from her, pointless and unhelpful.

"Oh, Mark, I wish we hadn't come. It was all a mistake, I want to go ho—"

The words faded into a gasp as she saw it.

"Wow, look at that!"

Mark's voice was reverent. Julia looked with every fibre of her being.

What a view. What a wonderful, panoramic, glorious, indescribably beautiful view.

The sea, shimmering wherever their eyes turned, was a still as a pond. It lay before them across the road, down the hillside, so near they could almost touch it, satin smooth and sensuous. The impression was a reds and pinks and purples and golds, streaked and billowing across the darkening canvas of sky; then they saw that here and there, the fading sunlight glinted golden off the surface of the water, like gilding on the frame of an ornate old mirror. The smooth surface was broken occasionally by a silent, distant fishing boat. In the centre a small islet rose alone from the calm stillness, its murky shadows accentuated by a glimmering white building with a white pathway that meandered idly down to the shore. On the far horizon a vague, misty, dark purple shape suggested a quietly sleeping land mass: the neighbouring island.

As they stood there drinking it in, delicious evening scents drifted across, stealing into their consciousness, unidentified, exotic, triggering memories that were no more than vague feelings for Julia. As she gazed in wonder at the feast before her, she suddenly thought of her sketch-book, packed in secret hope at the bottom of the suitcase; and it seemed that from her head to her shoulders, from her shoulders through her body, down her legs through her feet and out into the heady evening air, the fears slipped silently, never to return. The tension drained away, the tiredness was banished, the nightmare journey faded into insignificance, and Julia remembered why she had returned. It was going to be all right.

She reached for Mark, the key ready in her hand.

"I think this is ours," she said.

Leaving the Ancient Rose Castle

From a distance, the old castle resembled yesterday's birthday cake. The top of it was crumbling away, like buttery yellow sponge crumbles under sticky fingers, whilst the sides seemed to be held together by the wonderful wild rose that grew thickly round it. It looked like a greedy boy had come and broken a turret or two off and eaten them, leaving the sugar flowers in distaste.

Prince Florimund – or Rory, as he liked to be known – climbed up the uneaten South Turret, biting his lip. The state of the castle didn't bother him; he hadn't seen the outside of it for ten years, so the fact that it was falling down only came to his notice when it rained; and this being Fairyland – where anything can happen, and not all of it beneficial – it only ever rained at night.

"**Buckets!**" he would cry, from under his feather quilt.

"**Buckets!** Buckets! Buckets! Buckets! Buckets! Buckets!" he would hear, echoing down from the North Turret (mostly uneaten) in which was his bedroom. Then he would wait, sometimes getting soggy, sometimes playing Dodge the Drips, depending on how awake he felt. He knew that it was no use trying to rush things. Down in the bowels of the castle, the lowest of the low kitchen boys would dash to gather as many receptacles as possible: and one by one they would be handed up the ranks (scullery maid – boot boy – ostler – under footman – head footman – butler – personal valet – Rory).

Once, sensibly trying to save himself a wetting, he had intercepted the buckets on their way up.

"Here, quick, give 'em to me," he'd cried, snatching the rusty old iron things from the under-footman's hand.

"Certainly, Your Highness," uttered the underling, not betraying his feelings by even the flicker of an eyelid: but

136

the butler and the personal valet had not spoken to him for three weeks afterward.

Now, as he was slowly climbing the stairs to the South Turret, Prince Rory wondered what *her* reaction would be to the tradition he was currently breaking. It was so difficult to know what was best.

"After all," he thought, "what can she do? Throw me out?"

He laughed derisively. The sound echoed round the spirally stone steps of the turret, sounding terribly loud in the narrow space. He hesitated a moment on the final curve, waiting, his heart in his mouth. Had he got away with it?

No.

Sure enough, *she* had caught the sound. He flinched as the door opened at the top.

"Who's that?" she demanded.

"Only me, Sweet."

"Oh Florimund," she cried, "I'm sorry, I thought I heard someone *laughing*."

She peered down at him. "I was afraid I was going to have to order another head chopped off."

Rory was careful not to smile at her.

"No dear, that won't be necessary." He wondered how many servants they would have if he had carried out all her head chopping orders. Fortunately for the collective necks of the castle staff, Aurora rarely ventured outside the door of her room.

"No," she agreed, "I must have been mistaken. Were you coming to see me?"

"Yes," he replied, "but I can reschedule if now's not good for you… How are you feeling today?"

"I don't know why you even bother asking," she said. "You must know the answer by now. What's that in your pocket?"

Startled, Rory glanced down at his hosen.

"Not there! In your top pocket, idiot!"

"Oh – ah – this?" The golden envelope he had slipped into the top pocket of his coat had worked its way up and was peeping out, showing the loopy writing on it.

"Well – ah – I was just coming to show it to you, but perhaps—"

"Oh, *do* stop pussyfooting around," she cried, suddenly impatient. "If you've got something to show me just do it, will you?"

"Of course, my Cherub," he crooned, his heart sinking into his boots. She was in *that* kind of a mood. Sighing inwardly, he climbed the final few steps and entered the South Turret room, closing the heavy wooden door behind him.

The room was not inviting. There were black gauze hangings at the windows which kept most of the light at bay. The stone floors were cold and hard, unrelieved by carpets. There was a lumpy bed covered in ticking, with the remnants of what had been a canopy over it. The only other piece of furniture was a chair on which rested an ancient drop spindle, covered in cobwebs. It was a dark, threatening presence in one silent corner.

"Aurora, don't you think it would make you feel more cheerful if you let in a little light?" asked Rory, twitching one of the black drapes.

"I don't *want* to be more cheerful."

"You won't be able to see what I've got."

"Oh, very well, if you must," she grumbled.

Rory pulled back the curtain, letting in the dull light. Despite the fact that the window was covered in dense greenery, meaning very little daylight could worm its way through, Princess Aurora covered her eyes with her hands, groaning. Rory approached her, and taking her hands in his, gently pulled them away from her face.

138

"Sweetheart, how will you be able to see the ticket if you have your eyes covered?"

Taking the golden billet out of his pocket he waved it in front of Aurora's face.

"Owww," she moaned, closing her eyes. Then she opened one of them, squinting.

"Ticket?" she said. "What ticket? Ticket for what?"

Rory smiled. "It's for the People's Charity Ball at Princess Ella's. We've been sent VIP tickets."

"How did you get hold of those?"

"Fairy Starlight brought them."

"Starlight. That fairy is always trying to get me to go out. You'd think she of all people would understand."

"I really appreciate what she does for us. She's the only one that can get past the thorns. And without her, you know, we wouldn't have met."

Aurora sniffed. "She should have left well alone. Sometimes I think I'd be better off dead."

"But I don't. What would I do without you? Come now, darling, don't you think you'd like to go dancing? We could practice first, here in your room, so that you'll be quite confident."

"Whose ball is it? Princess Ella, did you say? You don't mean that commoner Cinder Ella, do you?"

"I thought she was the daughter of a baron? But whatever, she's the people's darling now."

"I don't care. When I first woke up to this wretched century, she was nothing but a kitchen maid."

"Darling, you know perfectly well she's royalty now. Prince Charming's wife and all that. It's not like you to be so... so..."

"Yes?" she said.

"Judgmental."

Aurora stared at him. Then she lowered her eyes and

139

plucked at the bedclothes, which started to disintegrate in her hands.

"Don't do that," said Rory, placing his hands over hers, "otherwise you'll have to have a new quilt, and you know how much that would upset you."

Aurora snatched her hands away. "Why are you torturing me? You know how little I have left – how little of my life is…"

"I know, I know darling, and you're such a brave girl. But one day, you will have to let go of the past. One day, you'll feel confident enough to step outside the castle grounds once again and face up to your new reality. I thought this might be a good excuse." He indicated the ticket. "You could get a new dress. I hear Ella uses that new designer – whatsisname – Rumpelstiltskin. Apparently he weaves straw into gold cloth. I think you'd look amazing in it."

"But Florimund, what are you suggesting? You *know* we never go out. It just isn't something we do. Besides—"

"It's been ten years, Aurora. I just thought it was time for a change."

"Change! CHANGE?! After all I've been through, you want me to embrace change? I have no energy to spare to change anything, not even my clothes. And anyway, what makes you think I'd be seen dead at one of that bimbo's shindigs? I do have a modicum of taste, you know! And you can stop waving that tacky gold paper at me. I'm not going, and that's final."

"Fine. But I warn you now, Aurora, I won't be kept a prisoner here. If you won't come with me, I'll go by myself."

"You'll what?"

"I'll go alone. By myself. Without you."

Rory didn't know what effect his rebellious words

140

would have. He half hoped there would be tears and tantrums, anything to put life into his beloved's eyes, but Aurora just stared at him. For a moment, he thought he saw a flicker of something, but it quickly died away, and she sighed.

"If that's what you want, then go. I won't stop you. Mind the thorns on the way out." Then she sank back on the bed and buried her head under the covers.

"Oh, and Florimund," came the muffled voice, "close the curtains before you go, will you?"

Rory went to obey her, but as he took hold of the dark curtain his hand seemed to ball into a fist of its own volition. He stood there for a moment, considering; then he rent the curtains down from the window so they couldn't be closed.

"No. Aurora, just let me ask you this. What was life like in this castle before you fell asleep? What were your Mama and Papa like? Would they be proud of this Princess Aurora? Would they approve that she doesn't wash or change her clothes? Would they like that she spends every day in bed?"

Aurora sat up slowly. Rory held his breath. She was responding! She leaned down and picked up the nearest thing, which was a plate with some mouldy cheese on it.

"How dare you! Get out. Get out of my room. Get out now, you... you... you...!" She lobbed the plate at Rory's head as hard as she could, before flopping down on the bed and bursting into noisy tears.

Rory stalked down the stairs, wiping mouldy cheese off his face. That was it, he'd had enough. He went to his leaky turret, took out his finest doublet and hose, and taking a heavy cloak for protection against the thorns, he left. The ostler, whose equestrian duties had dwindled to feeding and brushing Prince Florimund's steed – one of the few beasts that remained in the stables – looked up from where he was turning the spit in the kitchen as Florimund burst through the door.

"My horse – and be quick about it."

"B-but sire, where are you going?"

"I," said Florimund, "am going OUT! Find my sword, is it sharpened?"

The ostler had nothing better to do with his time; he sharpened it every day. He nodded, getting it down from the wall.

"Give it to me, and I shall have at these thorny roses. They may be sweetly scented, but they shall be my prison no longer."

The scullery maid screamed; Cook dropped the pan she was holding and the dog started barking.

"Sire – Prince Florimund – you're really going out? You mean – *out* out?"

Florimund, every inch the handsome prince, swept the sword from its scabbard and strode to the door. "Get my horse, boy. Get Silver Shield saddled and harnessed. It is time for change!"

Upstairs in her room, Aurora wept huge gulping sobs into her pillow. Rory's words had brought vivid memories, like the clearest pictures, to her mind; pictures of a loving Mama, and a Papa who liked nothing better than to go out riding with her. Pictures of the castle when it was full of light and life; musicians and dancers, courtiers and their ladies, beautiful clothes and mighty feasts. There were no crumbling turrets then, just gilded figurines. There was no briar rose, except for the one in the beautiful, cultivated gardens. She remembered the glorious, tiled fountain in the Entrance Courtyard, where she used to tease the dogs by throwing a ball into the water, and they would splash about chasing it, wetting not only themselves but whomever was within a few yards of them. Oh, what golden, halcyon days they were. Gone now, all gone. And it was all her fault.

That fateful day, her parents away on kingdom business, she'd been bored of playing with her friends. Although it was raining and there was nothing to do, she had petulantly dismissed her playmates and had decided to explore the creepy east wing of the castle. It only contained a few storerooms, but Aurora liked to pretend it was haunted. Nobody had ever disturbed her before when she ventured there, so it was with great surprise that she had found an ancient crone working away in the topmost room, on what she now knew was a spindle. Perhaps she ought to have thought it through, for it was an unusual circumstance; but she was used to the unusual in Fairyland, where anything could happen – and not all of it beneficial. Fascinated by the thread the woman was producing, Aurora had drawn near, curiously.

"What are you doing, Madam? What is this magic?"

"No magic, your Highness," said the old woman. "This is spinning. Any woman in the kingdom can do this for herself; and having spun the thread, can weave it into a fabric to make gowns."

"Spinning!" Aurora had shrunk back. "Is this then a spindle? I am forbidden to come near it."

"Really? Who tells you such nonsense? There is no more satisfying craft than spinning. See – see how the raw fleece forms into a single thread. It strengthens it, you know, so it can be woven into cloth. Would you like to try?"

"I – I'm not supposed to go near a spindle. I'm not quite sure why, but it's dangerous for me. I might prick my finger and die, or something."

"What a load of melodramatic nonsense," said the old lady. "How can it hurt you? There is no needle on here, simply a hook to hold the thread. Someone is trying to stifle your creativity. Come, let me show you."

Aurora didn't really know what stifling her creativity meant, but it sounded pretty bad; so slowly, she had drawn near. As far as she could see, there was no sharp point on the wooden stick the old woman proffered.

Gingerly, she took hold, trying to copy the way the woman had been holding it.

"No, no, not like that. You must be firm, or when you put the tension on, the spindle will fall from your hand."

The woman took Aurora's hand and wrapped it around the spindle.

"Ow!"

Too late, Aurora saw the sharp splinter sticking out from the wood, right where the woman had placed her hand.

"Oh dear. Has it drawn blood? Oh, look, yes it has. What a pity." The old crone threw off her cloak and started cackling, like the evil witch she was. "For all the care they have taken, I, Fairy Nightshade, have triumphed yet. Goodbye, foolish wench. You should have listened to your elders."

That was the last that Aurora knew, until she had awoken to find Prince Florimund, her darling Rory, bending over her. She could feel the residual heat of his lips on hers, and for a moment it had shocked and excited her; but she soon discovered she had opened her eyes on a changed world, a world without parents, without her old friends, and it rapidly put all other thoughts out of her head. Only the dogs and the servants had survived, all within the castle, having been protected by the mitigating spell of the twelfth fairy. Rory had explained her own story, now a legend, to her. He had cared for her, and nurtured her; and although she loved him, in the ten years they had been trapped together in the castle she had spiralled down and downwards.

For her, the century that had stolen all familiarity from her was but a night. The steady degeneration of the castle, which had begun the moment the spell was broken; the darkness caused by the briars; the crumbling towers, leaky roof and rotting draperies compounded a shock from which she felt she would never recover. Bewildered by these dreadful circumstances and wracked by guilt that her disobedience in touching the spindle had brought them about, she had dwindled into her room, tucking the darkness around her like a cocooning prison of safety.

Now, finally, Rory's words had set off an avalanche of grief. Rory, who had always been so patient and understanding with her. Rory, who had given her space and treated her like a treasure. Her darling Prince Florimund had finally snapped and was now abandoning her within her shrinking walls.

Well overdue, her tears soaked through the ticking on her bed. She cried for her parents, dead for many years. She cried for her playmates, who had lived and died whilst she was sleeping. She cried for her familiar world, all, all disappeared overnight and with the passing of the years; and she cried for herself; for poor Princess Aurora, adrift in a time not her own, where all she had become was a notorious relic from the past.

Eventually, her sobs ceased. The light at the window, though dim, was increasing even though it was early evening. She pulled herself up from her pallet and went to pick up the curtains.

"Florimund!" she said, looking out of the window. She could see him struggling against the briars. They were slowly giving way as he was working his way out.

She admired not only the determination with which he

fought against the thorny rose, but the way his muscles rippled under his fine linen shirt, his cloak thrust behind him. For her, he had fought his way through them into the castle, defeating their tenacious spikes. Wounded, he had wandered through the cold corridors until he found her. Finding her, he had tried giving her the kiss of life, not knowing that True Love's Kiss was the only thing that would break the thirteenth fairy's spell. That's how Aurora knew that he truly loved her. She put her fingers up to the window.

"Rory," she said, softly.

She went into her dressing room. How she hated to see her beautiful dresses all disintegrated, but now that the holding spell no longer protected them, they had faded and crumbled, giving way to moth and dust; all but one gown, which survived simply because it was made of gold cloth. And therein lay her deepest fear. For if the castle and everything in it, down to her very garments, could not survive the breaking of the spell, then what would happen to Princess Aurora if she went outside? Would she disintegrate? Would she wither and die?

She shook her head, suddenly realising that her worst fear was happening anyway. "I don't want to live like this. Live? This isn't living! It isn't even existing! It's only another kind of death!"

Taking a deep breath, she took the heavy golden gown and held it up.

"I can do this," she said. "I can. I must."

Rory was miserable. The charity ball was a complete disaster. Prince Charming was drunk; Ella was absent; her awful sisters Marlene and Charlene were persistently obnoxious and there was nothing he liked to eat. Trying to hide from the gruesome twosome, he bumped into Fairy

Starlight, who of course wanted to know why Aurora wasn't there.

"We – er – we had a rather heated discussion about the leaky roof. It doesn't matter how often I get up there and mend it, it crumbles again."

"Does it? Hmm. That doesn't sound right. I still don't understand why my mitigating spell hasn't worked properly. All should be back as it was before Aurora picked up that wretched spindle."

She tutted. "After all my efforts ridding the kingdom of them, that wretched Nightshade had to go and rob Rumpelstiltskin of the one he had hidden away, otherwise none of this would ever have happened."

She pondered as she tapped her chin.

"Perhaps it's not my spell that isn't working, but the breaking of Nightshade's spell that isn't quite complete. It's her power that would have had the castle crumble away; it's mine that was the holding spell that kept everything shipshape whilst the Princess was slumbering. Now that the holding spell is off, everything should have returned to its original setting."

"What, even her parents? She has taken their loss quite hard, Starlight."

"No, I'm sorry, not her parents. Even I can't bring the dead to life, Florimund. Depressed, is she?"

Rory nodded, miserably.

"Is that the real reason she isn't here?"

Rory nodded again.

"I can't get her to do anything, Starlight. She just lies in her bed day after day. It's been ten years of misery. If I bring her roses for her room, she just mutters that they'll die. If I try to get her to eat, she claims she's not hungry. Most days, she just berates me for having woken her up; and I can't say I blame her. It's no life, is it? Poor darling.

No, this is no good. I love her. I can't leave her. I'm going back. This party was a mistake, but thanks for listening. Goodbye, Starlight, I doubt I'll see you, unless you call at the castle again. My place is at Aurora's side, no matter what."

"Nonsense, boy, I'm coming with you. I may find some way to help."

Rory went to find Silver Shield and together they made their way back to the Castle.

As Aurora, stunningly clad in the cloth-of-gold gown, stepped out of the castle entrance and began to lead her rather shocked, plump little pony down what had been the carriageway, the briars shrank back behind her. With each step she took, they melted away as if they had never been. As she passed the broken down, dry, fountain, her tears began to flow again. She paused. This had been her favourite place; but so intent was she on escaping the castle that she didn't hear the tinkling sound of water beginning to flow through its pipes and out onto the magically restored tiles as her feet pressed on forward. As she reached the rusting iron gates, one of which was hanging off where Florimund had hacked his way through, they creaked open by themselves, the hanging one dragging noisily across the flagged courtyard entrance; then they both closed behind her as smoothly as the day they were made. She paused, taking a deep breath. This was the beginning of the end. Whether she survived or not, Aurora would no longer be a prisoner.

Behind the golden-clad figure, the turrets built themselves up; the gilding on the figurines shone forth. The gardens returned with their shady nooks and neat arbours. The breaking of the thirteenth fairy's spell was now complete. Unaware, the Princess mounted her grumpy pony and headed towards Prince Charming's castle. She had not gone far when she saw Florimund galloping towards her, Fairy Starlight clinging on behind him.

"Who goes there?" he called.

"It's me! It's me, Aurora. I decided I was coming to the party after all."

"Aurora! Oh, I'm so pleased to see you!"

Florimund came to a halt in front of her. They all dismounted. Then Rory looked up, and his jaw dropped in awe.

"What have you done? How did you do that?"

Aurora laughed, nervously. "What, the dress? It's one I had already. I—"

"No, not the dress," said Starlight. "He wants to know how you did that." She pointed behind Aurora.

Aurora turned, and gasped as she saw her home restored to all its former glory.

"*I* did that? Me?"

Starlight nodded.

"It must have been you. You were the subject of Nightshade's spell, and of the mitigation I put on it."

Starlight sat in thought for a moment. "Ohhh, I see. Yes, I get it now! Not only did Florimund have to work his way in and kiss you—"

"Without consent," muttered Aurora.

"I know, I'm sorry, I thought you were dying, so I gave you the kiss of life. Do you really mind?"

"No. No, because it *was* the kiss of life. You're right, it really was. And anyway, if I'm honest... I liked it."

"Did you? You never said."

Rory and Aurora were moving closer and closer to each other.

"Well, I'm saying it now. In fact, I think I might need the kiss of life again. Shall I collapse on the ground in a faint?"

"No need for dramatics," said Rory, lowering his head towards her.

Fairy Starlight cleared her throat.

"If you don't mind, as I was saying... not only did Florimund have to overcome the thorns on the way in, you, Aurora, had to brave them and come out! Only then would the spell be completely broken. You see, it may only have been a technicality, but some of these little details can be incredibly powerful..."

But Rory and Aurora weren't listening.

About the Author

Dawn Bush trained as an actress before putting her career aside to concentrate on bringing up her two daughters. She started writing as a creative outlet, initially crafting stories for her children and later adapting Bible stories for performance in her local church. After her children left the nest, she returned to acting and writing as a career. She has adapted three novels for the stage, two of which toured successfully; the third, a musical, is in the early stages of production. She writes songs, comic poems, flash fiction and monologues as well as short stories. She lives in leafy Warwickshire with her husband, where she enjoys dancing, gardening and long walks by the reservoir.

Like to Read More Work Like This?

Then sign up to our mailing list and download our free collection of short stories, *Magnetism*. Sign up now to receive this free e-book and also to find out about all of our new publications and offers.

Sign up here:
http://eepurl.com/gbpdVz

Other Writing by Dawn Bush

The Author's And
Published by Austin McCauley

Have you ever felt you didn't quite fit in? Well, that's how Jo felt. She was well-meaning, ordinary and a bit clumsy; and she lived in the middle of a perfect family. Although Jo wasn't the brightest button in the box, she could see clearly that Jesus had missed her out in the talent stakes. Luckily though, one thing she did have was a mum who wrote stories; and it was through those stories that Jo began to understand that she was actually very important perhaps even the most important person in her family.

Follow Jo as she discovers the beauty of words and the magic of fairy tales, and why And is so very necessary to the Author's book.

"*The Author's And* is a beautifully written story for children to illustrate the Christian message in a lively and imaginative way. It has beautiful illustrations too." (*Amazon*)

Order from Amazon:

Paperback: ISBN 978-1-398411-86-9
eBook: ISBN 978-1-398404-32-8

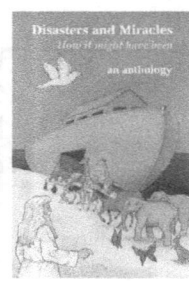

Samuel's Miracle in
Disasters and Miracles
Published by Bridge House (2009)

Order from Amazon:
Paperback: ISBN 978-0-9557910-4-8

Other Publications by Bridge House

For a Few Hours

by Yvonne Walus

Would you ever hire a sex worker, go all the way to New Zealand to join a man who may or may not be the love of your life, or shield your sister from going to jail by taking her place instead? And when you're a boy longing for sex with your girlfriend, what would you do when the earth literally moves and you have to face the consequences of a major earthquake?

For a Few Hours is the new story collection from Yvonne Walus, whose unforgettable characters are bold, vividly portrayed, and make you wonder about their choices and what you would do in their shoes.

"This is a tremendous collection of short stories. A great variety of themes and perspectives, with something for everyone." (*Amazon*)

Order from Amazon:

Paperback: ISBN 978-1-914199-20-2
eBook: ISBN 978-1-914199-21-9

The Memory Keeper

by S. Nadja Zajdman

In these eighteen linked stories, the reader accompanies our heroine Noela ("born on Santa Clause's Day!") as she develops from an insecure Daddy's Girl into a woman willing and able to stand on her own. Go on this journey with her as she meets challenge after challenge and as her relationships with all around her change.

The Memory Keeper is a collection of tales about a life well learnt in S. Nadja Zajdman's distinctive story-teller voice.

"A really lovely collection –I'm going to read mine again."
(Amazon)

Order from Amazon:

Paperback: ISBN: 978-1-914199-18-9
eBook: 978-1-914199-19-6

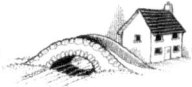

www.ingramcontent.com/pod-product-compliance
Lightning Source LLC
Chambersburg PA
CBHW071344170626
46811CB00003B/982